THE RAVEN

AND

THE PRISM

BY

JOSEPH

BENCIC

COPYRIGHT © 2013 JOSEPH BENCIC

1

Red and orange leaves drifted on the soft breeze. The air smelled of horse, and decomposing foliage. The setting sun cast deep shadows on the muddy forest road. Randall glanced up to the violet sky as a raven glided under wispy clouds. He pointed out the bird to Tar, a fellow squire who was riding beside him. Both boys smiled at the good omen. While many men saw the black bird as an ill sign, warning of bad tidings or even death, the boys saw things differently. They were squires of Clan Raven, a proud and noble house. To them, the clever and crafty raven was a part of their identity.

Their host was six days out of Greenvale, riding home after the great autumn tournament. Most of the forty riders had conflicting emotions regarding the tournament results. Sir Forrest, the knight that Tar squired for, reached the fourth round in single combat. This was quite a feat, considering the strength of his competitors. Randall squired for Sir Darwyn. Darwyn placed second in the joust, which was the best showing for Clan Raven in twelve years. His efforts earned him a bag of silver, and a prize-winning turkey for next month's harvest festival.

Their mood changed, however, during the grand finale. The melee is the traditional end to the autumn tournament. It is a chaotic and dangerous battle royal between thirty knights. Most combatants wear heavy plate mail armor, yet some sacrifice that protection to gain speed, and choose lighter chain mail or even leather armor. If a combatant takes three hits, or is knocked down once, he is removed by a referee. Last man standing wins.

There were always accidents in the melee, and this year was no different. Nine men injured, four dead. Sir Edwood was the pride of Clan Raven, and Lord Claypool's favorite nephew. He was expected to do well. He did at first, smiting the champions from Clans Toad, Unicorn, and Beaver in short order. It was his own supposed ally, that buffoon Sir Arlis from Clan Heron, who ended him. They were standing back-to-back; Edwood's greatsword and Arlis' mace keeping the field clear around them. Arlis reared back to crush an oncoming foe. The backswing of his mace caught Sir Edwood on the back of the head, and that was it.

One week past, and the pain of Sir Edwood's death was still fresh. Randall tried to stow it away. The time for grieving was done.

Lord Claypool called for an end to the day's march, and everyone got to work. As Sir Darwyn's squire, Randall's first duty was to raise Darwyn's tent. Next he gathered firewood to cook his master's dinner. Only after all his duties were done did he tend to his own needs. The life of a squire was hard, but it did have its rewards. Randall had been trained with sword and shield for eight years, since he was a boy of seven. Having Sir Darwyn as his mentor was a master class in courage and chivalry. Randall had become the most promising warrior of all the squires in Clan Raven, and the Elders had noted his sense of honor, as well.

Lord Claypool retired to his wagon to sup with his wife and son. The rest of the men, stewards and knights, horse boys and squires, ate together and drank wine into the night. The Ravenshields, Lord Claypool's personal guards, stood watch. As usual, many of them ended up joining the festivities and drinking with the rest of the men. After all, it was a time of peace, and they were traveling through friendly territory.

*

Was it some sound, or was it the chill that woke him? Either way, Randall had to pee. His tiny tent was not tall enough to stand in, so he was on his knees to strap on his sword belt. He glanced at his chain mail shirt, and then decided against it. After all, he was only going to the tree line to relieve himself, what could possibly happen?

Most of the campfires had gone to coals, still emitting heat, but not much light. A silver moon provided enough glow for Randall to find his way around the tents. The only sounds were soft snoring, and the occasional whicker from one of the horses tethered nearby. Randall found a likely spot a few paces past the tree line. As he was finishing up, he thought he heard voices coming from further in the woods. Going back to bed would have been the wise thing to do, but he no longer felt tired. He made a quick decision and started in after the voices, before he could talk himself out of it.

It likely wasn't anyone from Clan Raven, and there were no towns nearby. Perhaps it was bandits looking for easy prey. If so, they would not find Lord Claypool's host to their liking. The only other people in the area were the Bear Clan host, camped an hour or two further up the road. Sometimes clans would mingle on the way to or from a tournament, but not these two. Bear and Raven had bad blood between them that reached back generations. The autumn tournament did nothing to change that. Sir Corben had been Bear Clan's great hope for joust. He was embarrassed in his first ride, unhorsed by Sir Darwyn. Corben landed in dung and was kicked by his own horse. After that there were a few minor scuffles in the feast tents, forcing the Lords of both houses to order their men to stay among their own.

Randall found a game trail that led in the same direction as the voices. Walking silently was impossible with all the leaves crunching underfoot, but Randall was confident that he was quieter than those he pursued. He quickened his pace. More leaves on the ground meant less on the trees, allowing the moonlight to guide his way. The voices grew louder as he gained on them, and he found he could make out a word or two. It sounded like only two people.

They stopped walking suddenly, and so did Randall. Had they seen him? He doubted it, but slid behind a tree just in case. What was he doing? It wasn't too late, he could still turn back. Randall took a deep breath and headed toward the voices, walking stealthily among the shadows.

"…take too long. This is stupid," said a whiny voice. "I had to carry the thing. You should pluck it yourself".

"It'll go twice as fast if we both do it," said the other voice. "Besides, you'll catch a beating if you don't. Mutt wont hold back, you know that."

They were only boys, younger than Randall by the sound of them. He had an idea what they were plucking, as well. Feeling more confident, Randall strode toward them openly. He approached their backs without being noticed. About twenty feet ahead of them were two horses tethered to a tree. The boys must have ridden to here, then made it the rest of the way to the Raven camp on foot.

"This is stupid," said the whiny voice again. "Why do we have to pluck this thing in the middle of the forest anyway?"

"Because," Randall said boldly, "if you bring Sir Darwyn's prize turkey back to your camp with all its feathers in place, you will be known as the thieves you are, and will be punished."

The boys stumbled away from the newcomer; eyes wide and mouths open with terror. The whiny one shrieked and tripped over his own feet, dropping the bird as he fell.

"Now don't either of you think about running," ordered Randall, laying a hand upon the hilt of his sword. "The three of us are going to head back to camp together."

The boy on the ground was trembling. The other boy didn't seem nearly as scared, and his eyes momentarily darted to something behind Randall. In a heartbeat, Randall was drawing his sword and pivoting his body. It was too late. Something whooshed behind him. His right elbow screamed with sudden pain. His sword spiraled into the night.

Randall ducked as he turned to face his attacker. The blade of a spear sliced through the air where his head had just been. This fight was for real. Randall let his training take over. He grabbed the spear and pulled, using his assailant's own momentum against him. The assailant was bigger and stronger, and Randall's good arm was useless. There was no way he could win this fight. He had to get away fast. As the spearman stumbled past, Randall kicked the side of his knee. The man yelped in pain as he fell, but wouldn't let go of his spear. Randall ran past the boys, hopped onto one of their horses, and rode away quickly. His elbow hurt even worse with all the bouncing, but it didn't feel like anything was grinding together in there, so maybe it wasn't broken. That was good. From behind, a raging voice screamed "You are dead, Raven!" That was bad.

Even though he only saw his attacker for an instant, there had been something familiar about him. Everything happened so fast there was no time to ponder it, but that screaming voice brought his memory to the surface. That was Mutt, squire to Sir Corben of Bear Clan.

After ten minutes of riding full speed, Randall slowed his horse and steered her off the path. His head was muddled from the pain and shock. He hoped he was headed south, but couldn't be sure that he was. Finding his way back to camp was his only hope for survival, but he had lost all sense of direction. The sound of racing hoofs grew louder from behind him. Tucking his injured arm tight to his chest, he urged his steed to quicken her pace. The ground gradually inclined, and soon they were headed uphill, winding around maples and pines. Glancing over his shoulder, Randall saw movement in the trees thirty feet behind him. It was Mutt. The tip of his spear gleamed in the moonlight.

They were almost at the crest of the hill. Randall looked desperately right and left, hoping for a weapon or an escape, seeing only trees. Looking back again, he saw Mutt was nearly upon him.

"Told you I would kill you!" Mutt cried, throwing his spear.

Letting go of the reins, Randall raised his left arm to defend himself. That's when his horse dropped out from under him, and Randall was in the air. Time seemed to slow down. He was in mid tumble, heels over head. His horse was struggling mightily not to fall over the lip of the cliff. Mutt's spear sliced harmlessly through the air. Still tumbling, Randall saw the ground rush up to meet him.

His feet hit the dirt first, but the full impact never came, he only slowed down. The ground collapsed in a sudden sinkhole and he was falling again, into complete darkness. Then he was sliding, then rolling, and then he passed out.

2

Pain greeted Randall as he drifted back to consciousness. His hip, head, and arm were the worst, and his whole body felt bruised and battered. Opening his eyes, he saw only blackness. There were drips all around him; some rapid, some slow. Some hit rock with a *tic*, others *plooped* into shallow water. All produced curious echoes. Randall felt quite disoriented. He tried to sit up, but his injuries convinced him to lie back down.

The situation was bleak. Trapped in a cave, far under ground, with no light source. He had no water or food, water being the first priority. He had no supplies, the only thing he had was a sword belt with no sword. He reached down to the belt and felt around until he found the dagger hilt. At least that hadn't been lost in the fall. A dagger could mean the difference between life and death in a situation like this.

Randall didn't know how long he had slept, but his thirst was raging, so it must have been hours. The dripping sounds seemed to make the thirst worse. Rolling onto his belly and crawling forward, he hoped to find a puddle to drink from. He found one soon enough and bent down eagerly to drink. The putrid smell hit him like a slap, and he started to cough. The whole cave had a moldy, stale odor to it, but didn't compare to the sulfuric, tainted smell of the puddle. He crawled on until he found a different puddle, then another, but both were as putrid as the first. This water was poison, drinking it might slake his thirst, but would also hasten his demise. Instead he felt around for a steady drip and cupped his hand underneath it. He cautiously sniffed the water cupped in his palm. It seemed fine, so he took a tentative sip. Much better. He rolled onto his back and opened his mouth under the drip.

The finest nectar would not have tasted so sweet. Cold water splashed his face as he closed his mouth to swallow. For a brief moment, he was happy. There he lay, staring blindly at the ceiling of the cave, then gradually realized that he was *seeing* the ceiling, however faintly. That meant there had to be a source of light. Randall sat up, and the pain wasn't nearly as bad as he dreaded it would be. In fact, he felt much better than his situation warranted.

He looked around. Now that his eyes had adjusted, he saw a number of glowing patches scattered about the chamber. With a wince and a grunt, he stood. He was a squire of Clan Raven, one day to be a knight. If he were to die in this dark pit, it would be on his feet, like a man. He stumbled toward the nearest blurry glow, gradually regaining his balance. On closer look they were green glowing mushrooms, bioluminescent fungi.

Dropping to his knees, Randall drew his dagger. He slid the blade across the nearest mushroom cap, and an orange light shone brightly from the cut. He sliced through more of them, coating his blade with the strange glowing substance. Holding it aloft, it shined about half as bright as a torch. A shadow moved on the rock formation beside him and he slashed down with his shining dagger. It was a giant centipede, cut in half by the knife. Each piece was as long as Randall's hand, still wiggling. It was the most disgusting, delicious thing he had ever eaten. It crawled its way into his belly.

And so he survived. For three days he drank, and ate, and survived, in the cavern of his destiny. On the third day, he was strong enough to move on. There was a place at the end of the cavern where the floor sloped down into a narrow tunnel. Other than that there were only slippery rock walls, stalagmites, and poison puddles. He slashed his dagger through a batch of glowing mushrooms to brighten its light, and then set off down the tunnel. The going was easy at first, but the slope steadily grew steeper. He switched the dagger to his right hand so the stronger left could grab at the tunnel wall. His foot slipped on the wet rock, and there was nothing to grab. He slid down the muddy tunnel, and then he was falling again.

Bones crunched as he landed, but not *his* bones. Randall stood on a pile of animal skeletons, some so old they turned to dust as he walked. Others were alarmingly fresh. This cave was brightly lit by large, cone-shaped mushrooms. They glowed blue and were almost two feet tall. From a cluster at the center of the cave came a white light, blinding after days spent in darkness.

Something large moved to his left. He turned, raising his orange dagger, and it was upon him. Gnashing teeth and slashing claws, it was strong and relentless. It had a round body and six arms with humanoid hands, all covered in stout brown hairs. A horrible cross-breed of monkey and spider. Randall took four or five good hits before he regained his senses. For a time he parried incoming blows aside. Suddenly the six arms were moving as twelve, and the spider-thing fought with a furious strength. Randall was on his back, winded. The spider-thing's jaws were at his throat when his dagger found its home in the creature's heart. Rancid blood drenched his chest. He howled with victory, voice echoing back from rippled rock walls.

Randall stood in a crouch and pivoted, ready for anything. His eyes and ears were as attuned as they could possibly be. There were no more enemies here.

He gazed into the white light and saw a shape. Was it a bone, or maybe a giant tooth? Randall slid his dagger back into its sheath and reached for the bone with his right hand.

"Well met, sir," a voice said.

Randall jumped away from the sound, looking around wildly. "Who's there?" he called out in a shaky voice. It had sounded like someone was right at his shoulder, but he was the only one there. Surely he couldn't be going mad already, it had only been a few days. What else could it have been then, a spirit? Why would a ghost haunt this lonely cave when there were perfectly good ruins and bone yards on the surface?

Randall laughed, and listened to his voice echo back to him. Gazing at the white light at the middle of the cavern, he felt calm. Curiosity got the best of him, and he went back to examine the bone object in the center of the light. Pulling it out so he could look at it without getting blinded, he noticed it was longer than he thought. The bone was tapered, with a slight curve. At its wide end was an ornately carved scabbard. The bone was a sword grip.

"Sorry to have startled you," the voice said. It sounded ancient yet youthful, and had a curious accent. There was something else as well. It didn't echo.

Drawing the sword, Randall turned, knowing what he would see. Nothing. "Show yourself!" he demanded.

"I just did," chuckled the voice. "I bare myself to you, as naked as the day I came into this world."

"Who *are* you?" Randall asked anxiously. "An invisible imp, a spirit, what?"

"Are you always this dim, or did you hit your head when you fell down here?" mocked the voice. "Has your memory been affected, do you know your own name?"

"I am Randall Delaine, a squire from Clan Raven," an edge of anger was creeping into his voice. "And you are…?"

"Ah, a feisty one, this could be good," said the voice. "I usually only work with knights, but you will be one soon enough, I am sure. I am called Dragonwing; an Estragga blade forged at the height of the elven dynasty. I am one of the Nine, a group of mystical weapons created to protect this world. I have slept for nearly a hundred years, waiting for the next hero to wield me. Waiting for you".

Mouth agape, Randall stared at the sword in his hand. The weapon was beautiful, the workmanship exquisite. The blade was four feet long and deadly sharp. At the hilt it widened with three sharp wedges on either side, looking like stylized dragon wings. He slashed it through the air. The balance was perfect.

"A talking sword," muttered Randall.

"I do not speak," said the sword, "do you see a mouth on my blade? The words are in your mind, no one else can hear me."

"A voice in my head that only I can hear! Fantastic!" exclaimed Randall. "It would seem that I have gone insane after all."

"Perhaps," said Dragonwing with mock sincerity, "but I've only just met you. Give me a week or two, and I'll let you know for sure."

3

Rather than getting bogged down by the enormity of what he was experiencing, Randall decided to ask the first question that popped into his head: "You said you were waiting for the next hero to wield you. Why did you pick me? I've done nothing heroic… I am but a squire. Sir Darwyn is a seasoned warrior, a brave –"

"Yet you'll notice," interrupted the Sword, "Sir Darwyn is not the one stuck in the bowels of the Earth with an enchanted talking sword in his hand."

"Yes, but why?" asked Randall. "Why me? I'm no hero."

"You will be, or I could never have chosen you," replied Dragonwing. "How does the bee know how to make honey? How does the plant know how to flower? Does it matter? They were created to do these things, and they do them perfectly. *I* was created to do three things: to find a hero, then to find a demon gateway, then to close the gateway. That is how it happens, over and over. I do not know exactly how I chose you; remember, I am the *enchantment*, not the *enchanter*. All I know is that I have chosen perfectly each time".

That last part was not completely true, but the Sword didn't want to confuse his new friend.

Sitting cross-legged beside the blue mushrooms, Randall laid the sword across his knees. His right arm was sore, and the pain in his hip was also quite insistent. The most troubling thing, however, was how easy all this was to accept. It just felt *right*.

"Over and over," he muttered. "How many times have you done this?"

"You are the nineteenth wielder," answered Dragonwing.

"How…how old are you?" asked Randall.

"I was forged fourteen hundred and seventy one years ago by the mages of Clan Dragon, to protect the realm from incursion by monsters and demons from other worlds." The sword sounded proud of its history.

"So what happens next?" asked Randall, as he laid the sword on the ground. Something moved at the corner of his vision, and he turned to the mushrooms. A fat purple salamander was basking in the eerie glow. Randall quickly cut off the head with his dagger, then carefully sliced the belly and removed the guts. "Do we head straight to this gate?"

"We must train together, and become as one." The sword responded. "You must become a knight. But first, we must escape this cave."

Gnawing on the meager meat of the salamander, Randall looked over at the sword. He was no longer touching it, but the voice was still loud and clear. They were connected. "Alright, how do we get out?"

"You didn't think this was going to be easy, did you?" The sword laughed its odd laugh. "We must head down, to where this water-formed cave leads to a wyrm-tunnel. Wyrms were ancient reptilian creatures, giants who tunneled below the surface. They died out long ago, but their legacy remains. Various creatures of the dark use these tunnels as underground roadways.

"You are full of questions," continued Dragonwing. "Let us put those to rest for the moment. It is important for you to know that I am not only a weapon… I can also protect you. You are of Clan Raven, yes? I've never done a bird before, this should be interesting."

The sword told him to picture himself wearing a suit of armor, so Randall did. As the thought formed, he felt a weight on his chest. The pressure spread down his arms and legs. Ornate matte black steel plate armor appeared on his chest, arms and legs. Elbows, knees and all other moving bits were coated with small feather-shaped steel wedges, allowing full movement and full protection. A feathery black cloak flowed from his shoulders. The suit was relatively light, considering how much protection it obviously provided. His vision became slightly distorted, so he asked why.

"You are wearing a great helm," came the sword's response. "There are no eyeholes, thus no weak point. Others looking upon you will see the head of a raven, beak open, prepared to strike. The invisibility spell woven in the helm allows you to see through it, so there is no blind spot. As with the armor, you need only use your thoughts to don it or remove it."

Randall decided he didn't want to wear a helm at the moment, and felt it dissolve from his head. He took a few steps, and moved his arms around. The armor was very flexible, and didn't seem to impede his movement at all. Usually plate mail armor was heavy, and slowed the wearer considerably. He took a few practice punches. Amazingly, his punches felt faster and stronger while wearing his new armor. He realized that he just took a swing with his right arm without being walloped with pain. He flexed that arm at the elbow a few times. The injury was still there, but the pain had subdued to a dull ache.

"Your injuries will heal quicker while wearing the armor," said Dragonwing. "Their pain will also be reduced."

"Lets see about that," Randall said with a grin. He grabbed the sword and took his stance. Pause. Breathe. Then he was off, a blur of movement. He executed his advanced swordplay drills perfectly, as well he should, considering the amount of hours he had spent practicing in the training yard back home. Dodging, thrusting, slicing; his movements seemed more graceful and precise than they ever had before. He finished with a great arcing slice, accidentally lopping the tops off a few of the glowing mushrooms.

Blinding blue light filled the cave, along with a painfully piercing hum from the wounded fungi. Randall couldn't see, or hear, or think.

"Helmet on! Dim!" Dragonwing screamed in Randall's brain. As the helm appeared once more upon his head, Randall gratefully felt the sound reduced to a less incapacitating level. The blinding light also lessened, enough for him to see once again.

"It would seem we are no longer welcome here," said the sword. "Time to find our way down to the wyrm-tunnels."

Randall agreed wholeheartedly. There was no water in this cave; he couldn't have survived long here anyway. He strapped the scabbard to his back and sheathed the sword. Searching the perimeter of the cave, he soon found a cramped tunnel heading deeper into the earth. Taking hold of the rock, he gently lowered himself into the darkness.

4

Rippled rock walls flickered with yellow and orange from the dancing flames. The tantalizing aroma of sizzling meat filled the air. Randall had not eaten a proper meal in nearly a week. Even though it was only a plump rat turning on the spit, to him it smelled like a feast fit for a king. Finally he could bear it no longer, not caring whether the meat was fully cooked or not. His whole body rejoiced as he tore off a chunk and swallowed it down.

It was three days since he left the mushroom cave. The first day began with an hour-long descent. Other tunnels joined his, but he paid them little heed. His way was down. Finally he found himself with faltering grip, legs dangling into an unknown abyss. From the sound of the echoes, it was quite a large cavern.

"I believe others have come this way," said Dragonwing. "It is safe. You will have to have faith. Surrender control. You have to let go."

Randall's fingers gave out, making the decision for him. He fell thirty feet and landed in a tall pile of hay. He drew his dagger, which still gave off enough of a glow for him to find his way. Without his helm on, Randall could feel a soft but steady wind. The air was fresher than he had smelled in days.

If others used the hay pile as a drop-in point, no matter how infrequently that may happen, the prudent course of action was to move away quickly. Dragonwing said to head left, so Randall did. They covered a lot of ground before Randall needed to rest.

That first night, Randall asked about the sword's name. Why Dragonwing instead of a more fearsome part of the great beast's anatomy? Why not Dragonfang or Dragonclaw?

"Hold up your hands, fingers splayed," ordered the sword. "Imagine these growing from your back, greatly enlarged and elongated, with skin stretched taut between each finger. These are the wings of a dragon. My hilt is fashioned from the bone that would correspond to the tip of your thumb. The part of a dragon's wing that cuts into the wind. A dragon couldn't fly without me. I am the Dragonwing."

*

On the second day, Randall found the ruins. A few short, crumbling stone walls were all that remained of a long building. Dragonwing suggested it might have been a way station for ancient subterranean travelers. Randall found firewood, broken pottery, and an empty water skin.

It was later that day that Randall came upon a skeleton. Clad in armor that had long since gone to rust, the dead man lay against the rounded rock wall, rusty sword protruding from his chest. His satchel held a rope, flint-and-steel, and seven gold coins. Randall took the leather satchel and slung it over his shoulder.

That night Randall had a fire, finally easing the chill that had settled into his bones. He decided to ask about the sword's previous wielders. Dragonwing had mentioned that this was his first time 'doing' a bird. What did that mean?

"As I said before," began the sword, "I was forged by the mages of Clan Dragon. This was at the peak of elven dominance, when they reigned supreme. I was made for elven knights to wield, and so they did. My first fourteen knights were all elves from Clan Dragon. For them I created roaring dragon helms, dragon scale armor, and cloaks that resembled the wings of a dragon. Then came the fall of the elven dynasty."

Dragonwing fell silent for a time. Randall thought it was finished, so he nestled down to rest. Abruptly, it continued:

"After a long slumber, I returned to find the first of my human partners: Komtuz of Panther Clan. He was a magnificent beast. The next three were from clans far removed from each other. Mantis, Barracuda, Rhino."

Randall knew of Panther Clan, the others were foreign to him. He was starting to understand that he was part of something much greater than himself, something historic. This was the time for him to step up and be fully engaged. This was the time for him to finally feel fully alive.

*

On the third day he killed a rat. A plump rat like that needed sustenance, and Randall soon found it. A wagon stood in the ruts dug into the tunnel floor from years of wheels and hoofs. At its front were the skeletons of two beasts of burden, fresh enough that there was still a smell. Further on were four human skeletons with hands bound. All the bones were well gnawed by rat teeth.

Later, he sat licking his fingers, warm rat grease dripping down his chin. This night he decided to ask about the nature of the mystical gateway they needed to close. How could it exist, and how could it be closed?

"Once upon a time, there was an evil wizard," began Dragonwing. "He was a thrall for the greater demon Thulos. He became obsessed with opening a gateway to his master's world. He joined forces with alchemists and clerics, delving deeper into the dark magics than any other mortal had ever dared.

"They created a legendary item, an eternal key to the gates of destiny. They created the Prism of Thulos. My first knight was Sir Llarys, the greatest hero of his generation. Llarys fought his way through harpies and lesser demons. In a battle for the ages, he slew the evil wizard."

Dragonwing was created to nullify the prism. All Sir Llarys had to do was lay the blade against the foot-tall crystal pyramid, and the deeply woven magics would close the gate. But that was not the end of the story.

Through the ages, the prism would materialize to chosen sorcerers or dark priests. Some were too weak to use it properly; others were strong enough to add to its capabilities, giving the prism the power to open doors to multiple worlds. Every time this happened, the sword would choose a new knight to wield it, and the threat would be stopped.

5

The next day Randall came to a fork in the tunnel. A smaller offshoot headed down to the right, but Dragonwing insisted they stick to the main tunnel. Around this time, Randall first noticed the sound of horses and voices coming from somewhere behind him. Should he find somewhere to hide until the strangers passed? If they had ill intentions, if there were too many of them, his quest could end right here. On the other hand, it had been a long time since he had seen another person. They might even have food to share. That decided it for him. Randall sat down to wait.

Soon torches could be seen approaching from where the tunnel curved. Although he was scared, Randall resisted the urge to draw his sword. The comfort it would give him would surely be outweighed by the mistrust it could cause. He also left his helm off, thinking that a human face would seem more welcoming than a shadowy raven.

The caravan drew nearer. Groaning wheels and clomping hoofs echoed along the tunnel. Under these sounds, the newcomers were speaking in a tongue unfamiliar to him. When they were close enough to see their faces, Randall stood and waved, calling out a friendly greeting. The riders slowed, and their suspicious eyes were now all focused on the black knight who blocked their path.

Four large wagons, towed by shaggy oxen, were heavily laden with bundles and crates. Fifteen riders surrounded the wagons. The riders were all short and wide. Not fat, from the looks of them, but heavily muscled. They all carried large battle-axes. Most had shields slung to their backs. As they came to a halt in front of him, Randall realized they were not quite human. Bushy hair sprung from brows that protruded a bit too far. Strangely bulbous noses bobbed over wide lips.

"Dwarves," said Dragonwing. "Traders, perhaps, bringing goods to their mountain stronghold."

Randall was shocked. Dwarves were not real; they were creatures from children's stories. Even as a child he hadn't believed in them. Yet here they were.

A stout fellow in a green cloak broke off from the rest and approached Randall. The dwarf had a bushy beard that reached past his waist, and wore a horned great-helm. He spoke haltingly, as though he hadn't spoken the common tongue in a long time.

"What are you doing here, human?" the dwarf asked. "The Underland in't for your kind."

"I fell down a sinkhole," said Randall. "Now I just want to find my way back up." The dwarf nodded, his eyes fixed on Dragonwing's hilt.

"What's that bone on your back, boy?" the dwarf asked.

Randall drew the sword from its scabbard. The dwarf gasped, and some of the others back at the caravan started muttering excitedly.

"I seen that blade before. My Granpappy showed me history books when I was a boy. Most elf weapons are trash compared to dwarven steel, but that one is a wonder. Gave you a quest too, I'm sure. Just don't expect us to bail you out if things go to hell again."

Randall had no idea what that last part was about, and the dwarf continued before he could ask.

"There's a tunnel what heads upward, five days ride that way," said the dwarf; pointing his axe in the direction they were headed. "It'll be longer on foot. Do you have any food?"

Randall shook his head.

"Ack!" said the dwarf. "I'll catch trouble for this when I get back but…hang on."

The dwarf rode his pony to one of the wagons and rummaged for a few minutes. When he returned, he had a sack of salt beef and a large water skin.

"If by some miracle you do make it out of here, you tell no one of us, understand? If the Underland starts teeming with humans, I will find you, feather knight."

"I swear," said Randall. "By my father and by Clan Raven. I will not tell a soul."

The dwarf rolled his eyes and grunted, then handed over the provisions. The caravan rolled on, leaving Randall in darkness.

6

Randall was gorging. He was on his third strip of salt beef before the glow of the dwarves torches had faded. Wearing the magic armor seemed to dull the hunger pangs slightly, but not enough. Now that he had a taste, he wanted to eat and eat until his belly was fit to burst. The sword wouldn't let him.

"Stop it!" said Dragonwing. "That food needs to last you a week, maybe longer."

"Hef Mabah," said Randall. He finished chewing what was in his mouth, and then tried again. "Yes mother. Next are you going to remind me to wash behind my ears?"

Regretfully, he tied up the sack and ate no more. The sword was right, of course. Even if Randall could find the occasional rat or salamander to supplement the salt beef, it still might not be enough. Food and water both would have to be rationed carefully.

"Alright. What do you suppose the dwarf was talking about?" Randall took a sip of water to wash the salt from his mouth.

"Which part?" asked Dragonwing innocently.

"Ha! I'm sure you don't know," said Randall. "He said they wouldn't help out again if things went to hell. He couldn't have been talking about me, since we just met. So he must have been talking about you. How did he help you?"

"It wasn't him, it was his ancestors," said Dragonwing. "The dwarves. It was the first time, the only time in recorded history, when dwarves, elves, and humans all joined forces. United against a common foe."

"That sounds familiar," said Randall. "I think I heard a song about that when I was younger."

"I'm sure you did. Multitudes of songs were written about those events. The fall of the elves. The Demon War. Of course some would still be sung today." The Sword paused, as if to collect its thoughts, then continued. "It was over five hundred years ago, yet for me it seems so close. Sir Buryll was the one; he enlisted the dwarves to our cause. But I'm getting ahead of myself. First I should tell about the one that came before. The thirteenth.

"Once upon — wait, I've already used that one. A long time ago, in a faraway land, there was an Empire. The elves gave the world great advances in science, medicine, and magic. They turned your ancestors from barbarians into civilized men, and created the society you live in. At their peak, at the time of my forging, they brought peace and prosperity to the realm. But like a raging bonfire, or a comet streaking through the sky, their light had to fade sometime. Nine hundred years later the elves had become lazy and decadent. Many had lost their connection to nature magic. Many had forgotten their honorable history. They lived for gluttony and sloth, importing slaves so they could avoid manual labour. They knew all about actors in the theatres, and gladiators in the pits, but nothing of themselves. They were lost.

"I told you I always chose the correct knight to wield me. I lied. My thirteenth knight, Sir Floraghtin, was the wrong choice. When I awoke from an eighty-year sleep, I knew the next incursion would be somewhere near Vellastra, the elven capitol city. I decided to find someone close to where the gateway would open. Two of my previous wielders were Imperial Knights. Both were valiant and skilled. I had slept through the fall of the elven dynasty, and didn't understand its extent. I thought that the commander of the Imperial

Knights would be able to rise above the decadence of his people. I thought that he would be trained as his predecessors had been. I was wrong.

"Sir Floraghtin had a heroic personality, but a craven heart. I was in such a hurry, I didn't see it. I thought I had to rush to save the elven empire, not realizing that it had already fallen.

"The prism emits a certain dark energy that I can sense. I can usually tell which direction it is, and how far away. Location, however, is not the only important aspect of an incursion. Who is trying to do this, and why? When? Is anyone else helping him? Knowing these things could be useless, or it could be vital. Sir Floraghtin underestimated the value of knowledge, and underestimated the forces that would be gathered to stop him. I told him, warned him, but he wouldn't listen.

"He could have brought a force hundreds of men strong. Instead he brought ten knights. Also dancing girls, musicians, servants, and plenty of wine. It was just another diversion to them.

"When that barn burst into flames as the portal opened, they actually cheered. Then the fire demons came. Just a few at first, since only two or three could pass through the portal at a time. The elves scattered. Sir Floraghtin knocked down two musicians in his attempt to flee. An army of fire demons would enter our world within the hour, but Sir Floraghtin and his group were dead long before that."

"Wait, an *army*?" asked Randall, an edge of fear creeping into his voice. "You had him going against an army of demons? Is that what you have planned for me?"

"If we would have gotten there sooner, he could have deactivated the prism before the army came through," said Dragonwing. "But he took too long to get started. As for what you will face, I cannot know. Over the years, some of my knights have faced seemingly insurmountable odds, and emerged victorious. Sometimes, yes, facing an army of monsters."

"How can I possibly succeed against such odds?" asked Randall. "What if you chose the wrong guy again? I might be your second mistake."

"You are not a mistake," replied Dragonwing. "When you are ready, you will know. I have arrived early, to give you as much time as you need. I learned two very important lessons from my thirteenth warrior. First: to arrive well before the incursion, to give my wielder ample time to prepare. Second: to never use proximity to the event to guide my choice. So, for my fourteenth knight I chose someone far from Vellastra. In fact, Sir Buryll had been born across the Haunted Sea.

"Eighty years earlier, Buryll's grandfather, Lord Stelfus, embarked on a quest for the fabled bow of Kolara. He searched the Southern Isles before heading across the sea. His son continued the quest after Stelfus died. He searched Ghazz and then Qan-Tze, where he took a wife. Sir Buryll was born half elf, half human.

"Buryll was at sea when the gateway opened and Floraghtin died. Sir Buryll had finally found the bow of Kolara, and was headed for the Empire to return the bow to its rightful owners. Having been born abroad, he had no idea how far the elves had fallen. He was raised and trained in the old ways. That's why I chose him.

"I found him in a gaming house in the harbor of Rillato. He was playing tiles with dilettante lordlings, trying to win enough gold to buy horses and provisions for the journey to Vellastra. By his last game, the stakes had grown quite high. Lose, and have to pay all the gold he had won that evening, and surrender the boat he had arrived in (which wasn't, strictly speaking, his to wager). Win, and he would gain all that was in the merchant's safe. I put myself in that safe. Sir Buryll won the match.

"I felt the difference right away. Sir Buryll was the last from Clan Dragon, the last of elf blood, to wield me. And he was one of the greatest, on a par with Sir Lloras the legendary. Buryll could fight like no other. He was the best of his generation. His finest gift, however, was his ability to cut through the political morass of that era. Sir Buryll was treated as a long-lost prince, given gravitas by his possession of both the bow of Kolara and the legendary Dragonwing.

"In truth, the bow of Kolara was just a regular bow by this time. I `accidentally' absorbed its magic when my scabbard rubbed against it. When we are in the open air, and have some time, remind me about the bow.

"Anyway, Sir Buryll visited many human kings. He convinced the seven most powerful kings to join his quest to liberate Vellastra and the elven homeland. All the men asked for in return were autonomy and the right to expand their borders.

"Buryll also sought an audience with the dwarf prince, ending two centuries of silence between adversaries. He managed to convince the prince that if the elven empire fell to the demons, the rest of the world would soon follow.

"Thus the miraculous alliance was born, when Sir Buryll led his army of humans and dwarves into the elf lands. Pockets of elven resistance fighters joined the unified army. The legend was born of desperation. If all three races had not joined together, the world would surely have fallen to the demon hordes.

"The campaign lasted nearly eight months. We had many adventures and fought alongside many heroes. After our quest is done, I'll have to tell you some stories. It was an incredible time. The Demon War."

Randall sat silent for a while. It was a lot to take in. These tales of battles fought long ago made him pensive. The crazy dream his life had become seemed more real now. He was part of a proud and storied history.

"That's not the end of the story," said Randall. "What happened to the dwarves and the elves?"

"The dwarfs withdrew," said Dragonwing. "They decided that their fear of outsiders was well founded. They would never again trade or interact with elf or human. Apparently, they have thrived in their isolation. The elves are a different story. Most of them just disappeared. Vanished into the air. Most people think they all died. I prefer to think that they left this world for another, where they could re-learn nature magic and the old ways. The ones who remained all dispersed, blending in with the Humans."

Randall slept deeply that night. In his dreams, he was not one man, but many. He was a reflection, an echo of all those who came before. He was a hero.

7

Never before in his life had Randall seen this much carnage. Unfortunately for him, it wouldn't be the last time he saw such things. Nor would it be the worst. The caravan was destroyed. Bodies of dwarves and ponies spanned the tunnel. They had been there at least a day, and were starting to smell. Randall fell to his knees and lost his meager breakfast. There was so much death surrounding him. The tunnel suddenly seemed much smaller. The immeasurable weight of dirt and rocks overhead was bearing down on him. He had to get out of this tunnel soon. Had to see the sun, to feel the wind on his skin.

He stayed on his knees, picturing himself in the forest, breathing deep and slow. When he was ready, he opened his eyes and stood up. The bodies were still horrible to look upon, but he did it all the same. He had to survive this ordeal, had to make it to the surface. He searched the bodies and the caravan, looking for anything useful. Whoever attacked the dwarves had stolen most of their provisions, but not all. Randall found bread, cheese, and a water skin. The cargo seemed to be apples, pears, and rum. Most had been taken, but Randall found enough fruit to weigh him down. He even took a jug of rum.

There were a few bodies he didn't recognize. "What could you be?" he said. They were humanoid, about three and a half feet tall, with copper skin. Their brows were angular, their noses sharp. They looked like lizard people. They had scales instead of pores, and no body hair. The stuff that grew from their heads wasn't hair at all; it felt more like long thin fingernails. Each wore armor that was custom made for a creature that size and shape. That meant they were not scavengers, they had their own civilization.

"Kobolds," said Dragonwing. "A warrior race, they value swordsmanship above all else. Oftentimes, groups of kobolds will align with evil masterminds, lured by the promise of valiant battle for a glorious cause. They are not native to this world, but thrive in four worlds that I know of. Likely more. They have been used as pawns in previous incursions. I'm not sensing the prism. No gateway either. This may be a group that got stranded here in some failed attempt to breach the…" --a scuffing sound from down the tunnel interrupted Dragonwing. Randall dove behind an overturned wagon.

Peeking over the debris, Randall saw a kobold approaching. Just one. He waited until the creature was in position. Drawing his sword and donning his helm, he pounced.

Randall descended with a clumsy overhead swing that the kobold easily dodged. The creature responded with a slash to each of Randall's arms and two stabs to his chest before the squire could raise Dragonwing for a second strike. If it wasn't for the magic armor, Randall would be dead already. He knew it, and responded with fury. All his lessons about poise and patience were gone from his mind. The kobold parried gallantly for a time, but when the first blow broke through, it was all over.

"Congratulations!" said Dragonwing. "You've defeated a superior opponent by virtue of your size alone. If you had been the same stature, or if you didn't have magic armor, you would have lost."

"But I didn't lose," said Randall. "He was fast, but I still got him. Kobolds wont be a problem."

"Oh really?" said Dragonwing. "How many do you think it took to defeat fifteen dwarves? At least thirty. Maybe more. You know what you would do against thirty kobolds? You would die."

"Thank you for your confidence in me," said Randall, with a sarcastic edge in his voice. "Now I feel like I'm ready to conquer the world!"

"Don't mewl, boy!" said Dragonwing. "Learn! If you are lucky enough to face another kobold one-on-one, fight him on his terms. Use the skills you learned in the practice yard. Adapt to his style. Respect his prowess, and learn from it."

That's just what Randall did. The next day he ran into a pair of kobolds. The tunnel had had a gradual and steady incline over the five days since he first met the dwarves, now it grew steeper. Blending in with the shadows, Randall waited until the kobolds were separated before he struck. He slammed the rear kobold to the ground, knocking the wind out of it. Then he spun around to face the one behind him.

The little copper man dodged his slashes with ease. The kobold fought with an unorthodox style, attacking in unexpected ways.

Instead of clobbering him with blunt force, Randall decided to adapt. He followed his lessons, dodging and evading. He parried what blows he could, and struck back with proportionate force. When the second kobold awoke, Randall knocked his opponent out with a sharp rap to the temple. Turning to face the new enemy, he took three hits before he could bring the sword up to block. One of its daggers pierced armor.

Randall felt the rage rising in him again, but this time he managed to control it. Instead of lashing out with brute force, he searched for a weakness in his enemy's defenses. With subtle feints and lunges, he began to press the advantage. When the kobold fought through and re-took the advantage, Randall learned a lesson that all his hours in the practice yard could never teach. The kobold moved with a certain grace, very fluid, with no wasted movement. Perhaps it was only luck that Randall saw the kobold's blade dip on each leftward slash. Maybe it was something more, a newfound intuition. Either way, his blade struck true and the lizard man fell.

Randall spun to face the other kobold. The sudden stabs in his ribs and arms told him his opponent had already awoken. He decided to use the same technique again: adapt to his opponent's style, and then use it against him. The fight was much quicker this time. Randall found his opening in less than half a minute.

Once he decided to follow their trail, Randall wasn't surprised at all that it matched the dwarves directions for escaping the Underland. The kobolds were trying to get out, too.

*

It was nearly a day later that he found them. A narrow tunnel branched off from the main one. "A teenage wyrm's surface excursion," explained Dragonwing. The tunnel ascended steeply. Stone blocks had been laid in as a staircase centuries ago. Various side tunnels branched off. When he found one with the scent of kobold, a rich bouquet of peat moss and poop, Randall drew his blade and dashed to the shadows.

Following a throaty hissing sound, Randall found a small tunnel that lead to a cave. It was kobolds he was hearing; that strange sound was their language. He stood at the mouth of the cave, where he could face them one-on-one.

"Come face me, you craven stinking lizards!" cried Randall. "Lets see how you do fighting me one at a time."

"This is a horrible plan," said Dragonwing. "Completely reckless. I like it!"

Three kobolds already lay dead at the mouth of the cave. Randall was using both force and finesse. With odds like these, he had to take every advantage he could.

"Watch out for the shaman," said Dragonwing. "He'll be wearing furs instead of armor, and will be hurling magic balls of horrible in your general direction."

More kobolds fell, and even more, until the mouth of the cave was piled high and they had to stop to remove some bodies before they could resume their assault. Randall saw a shining globe approach out of the corner of his eye. As it hit, he felt his eyelids and his weapon grow heavy. Time seemed distorted. It was as if he was wading through syrup. He had to finish this before he succumbed to the hex. He stormed through the little kobolds, knocking them aside on his charge to the shaman. The lizard wizard hurled one last magic ball. Randall's skin burst into searing flame. The armor extinguished the fire before a scream could escape his lips.

The shaman died quick, and the rest soon followed. Randall fought like a man possessed. Dragonwing sang as it sliced through the air. Then it was done. Randall stood panting, splattered with blood.

"Now you see," said Dragonwing. "Now you know what you are, what you can do. Now you have seen the light."

8

Two days later, Randall did see the light. It was filtered through cedar boughs laid at the top of the tunnel. Even though he was exhausted, the light spurred him to full speed. Most of the food was gone, and rationing had taken its toll, but still he found a way. Then he was pushing through the boughs, gulping in the sweet air, basking in the light.

It was cold. The ground was covered in a light dusting of snow. After the damp chill of the Underland, Randall hoped for some warmth. What he got was the dry freeze of an early winter morning. Even so, it was perfect. The forest was silent. The hibernators and migrators were gone.

Dragonwing told him to head southwest, so Randall did. He could feel that it was the right way to go. Once he emerged from the Underland, a weight seemed to have lifted from his shoulders. All those tons of earth bearing down on him were gone. He was free. That weight was replaced by the reality of his mission. He had made it out, and the sword was still there. That meant it wasn't all a bad dream. The sword, and the responsibility that came with it, was real.

He had two pieces of salt beef, a pear, and a few swallows of water remaining. Water was the first priority, as always, so he spent some time gathering clean snow to melt for his water skin. Food would be a different matter. He wouldn't be staying in one area for long, so setting snares was out of the question. He would have to hunt, and hunting with a sword was out of the question. He could tie his dagger to a long stick to make a spear, but he had never hunted with a spear. Ravens hunted with bows, that what Randall had been taught.

"Hey, sword," said Randall. His voice was an intrusion in the stillness of the icy air. "You told me to remind you about a bow. I don't suppose one of your knights knew how to carve a bow and arrow with a dagger, because that information would prove useful right about now."

"You mock, but I can help more than you know," said Dragonwing. "I told you that I absorbed the magic from the bow of Kolara. You must follow my instructions exactly."

That's just what Randall did. He spent the rest of that day searching for the perfect alder, one that had a thick, unknotted branch that Dragonwing approved of. Randall trimmed it to a foot and a half, and then whittled away the bark, just as the sword instructed. The next day he found a frozen swamp. There he harvested some dried reeds. He wove a conical quiver, using vines and birch bark to finish it off. The details Dragonwing provided were exact, and Randall followed them to the letter. That night he finished the last of his food.

Next morning, Randall strapped the quiver to his belt. He was stiff with cold, he was grumpy and hungry, but he did not give up. He spent three hours gathering twigs: two feet long, straight, no knots. They were hard to find. Finally he had twenty, and Dragonwing said he was done.

"Done?" said Randall. "I have a basket full of sticks and a belly empty of food. You've wasted what time we had left."

"Find a game trail," said Dragonwing, "and I will show you."

Randall was lucky, it took less than two hours to find fresh deer tracks. He followed them until dusk, when he spotted a doe and buck drinking from a gurgling stream.

"Hold the alder stick in front of you, in your left hand," instructed Dragonwing.

Randall did as he was told, and smiled. So *this* was the magic of the bow of Kolara. In his hand was not an alder twig, but an ornately carved black bow with a silver string. He grabbed one of the twigs and notched it. The twig transformed into a black arrow. Its point was a three-pronged steel talon; raven feathers balanced its rear.

Randall fired, and even though he had never fired this bow before, his aim was true. He built a large fire, and spent the evening cleaning, gutting, and skinning the doe. Randall ate well that night, and was left with more meat than he could possibly eat before it spoiled.

Days passed, and Randall grew stronger. He listened to stories of Dragonwing's adventures. Tales of past glory were fascinating, but Randall got to thinking about what he may soon have to face. He thought that kobolds could prove to be the least of his worries. One night he asked what kind of enemies he might have to deal with. Dragonwing had no way of knowing, but could provide details of previous adversaries.

"It all starts with a demon, and the first was Thulos. He was an elder demon of great charisma and power. Demons were banished from this world aeons ago by Deities and Titans. After ruining their own worlds and building a mythology out of re-taking this one, many demons have dedicated their long lives to the task. Thulos found a way through, and influenced that long-forgotten wizard to create the Prism of Thulos. Isn't it strange that I never learned the name of the wizard who caused all this trouble? Anyway, Thulos was behind the first three incursions, and four later ones. He had armies of Harpies, Hobgoblins, and giant centipedes.

"The fourth incursion was caused by the dark cleric Garshamonn. He altered the prism so that it could summon other demons as well. Thus came the Shadow Walker. It brought wisps and melters. These shadow fiends cast havoc on our world. Even after they were vanquished and the gateway was closed, the winter lasted for sixteen months. It took a decade before the weather returned to its normal cycle.

"The Lizard King, Gorrom, was the first to keep the prism on his own world. We had to trek through a purple swamp under six moons, fighting drakes and tri-lors."

"Alright," interrupted Randall. "These are just words to me. What are drakes and tri-lors? What are wisps and harpies?"

"Drakes are vicious lizards as tall as a man. Tri-lors are rotund men with lizard features and three horns growing out of their head." Dragonwing sounded abashed. From then on, his descriptions were more specific and useful.

K'raz al Necros was a demonic death worshipper. His re-animated skeletons could only be defeated with fire. Magmonn was a greater fire demon that brought forth hellhounds. The demon could be dissipated with a spray of water, only to return a few minutes later, angrier yet smaller in stature. The dogs breathed fire, and could only be killed by piercing the heart. The Whisperer was a silent ether demon with mental powers and spells. The touch of Dragonwing's blade caused the Whisperer to dissolve. It would reappear a few minutes later and trace the sword by its magic trail. Escape was impossible until the sword was on its own world. Wisps were teleporting shadow butterflies whose touch infected with stoneskin plague.

Randall listened for hours, until he fell asleep. Again he dreamt of lives lived centuries ago.

9

Once he realized that he was in Raven territory, Randall walked quicker, and slept less. He was headed home, maybe for the last time. He was looking forward to seeing his brothers-in-arms again. The knights and squires of Clan Raven had been his only family for the past few years. He was less eager to see his father, who had sent him off to train shortly after Randall's mother and brother died. Since then, father and son had only seen each other at holidays and feasts. Milos was a hollow man. After his wife died, he had no love to give his surviving son.

Randall had started his training as an outcast, a motherless child from a common house. The other boys were all from noble houses, but the knights and men-at-arms treated all the squires the same. Over time, the boys formed bonds and became like family. Tar was his closest friend; the one Randall was most excited to talk with about all that had happened.

Walking through skeletal forests, skirting glittering ponds, Randall drew ever closer to Heston Hold. Three days after felling the deer, on a crisp windless morning, he could see smoke rising from the chimneys of a few outlying farmsteads. He made his way along a path that divided two fields: corn on the left, barley on the right. He came upon a small, sod-roofed cottage. A young man was chopping wood out back. When he saw Randall approaching he smiled, and laid down his axe. For a moment Randall wondered if it was someone he knew, but the man was a stranger. It was the armor, he realized. Of course someone in raven armor would be welcomed in these parts.

They chatted amiably for a few minutes, and the man shared his skin of wine. Since his farm was so far removed from Heston Hold, the man had no idea what had happened there. Even if he had known, even if he could have warned Randall, nothing would have changed. Nothing could have prepared Randall for what he was about to see.

Hours later, as the tangerine sun dipped into a cloudy horizon, he saw.

The narrow path from the croplands joined to a wider road. The road curved through a dense evergreen forest before emerging in the flatlands that surrounded Blackfeather Hill. Stomach fluttering with anticipation, Randall rounded the last curve. His heart sank.

Heston Hold stood as it always had. A wide, stout castle surrounded by black stone walls. From its place atop Blackfeather Hill, the castle provided a great view of the surrounding area. At the base of the hill was a small army, perhaps five hundred men. Randall was shocked. Heston Hold hadn't faced a siege in hundreds of years, since the unification. They were much too far north for the Southland barbarians to reach. They had no coastline, so they never had to worry about pirates, either.

Each knight and soldier had to serve at least two years in the King's army, patrolling the eastern or southern coasts. Some chose to stay, lured by the steady pay or the promise of adventure. Most returned home. Randall knew that some of them, like Sir Darwyn, had served time at borderland castles, defending them from raids. He hoped that would be enough. Most of Clan Raven, including Randall, had only a rudimentary knowledge of how to defend their home from a siege.

"Go!" said Dragonwing urgently. "Hide! Now!"

Randall snapped back from his reverie. Hoof beats were rapidly approaching. He scrambled into the bush and dove behind a wide cedar trunk just as four riders came into view. He lay perfectly still, focused on quieting his rapid breathing. There were no shouts, no sound of blades being drawn from scabbards. He hadn't been seen.

He donned his raven helm, knowing the black would help him blend with the shadows. He peeked around the tree, moving slowly to minimize the crunch of dead leaves under the thin blanket of snow. The riders had stopped and dismounted.

"Chances of finding one are slim," said a man with a bow. "I haven't seen much game since we arrived. They probably hunted these woods bare years ago."

"I'm sure they did," said another man. This one was heavy, with a broadsword strapped to his back. "But Willins said that Lord Kodiak had a craving for venison, so it's hunting we go. Do you want to go back and tell him no?"

"No sir," said the archer.

"That's what I thought," said the big man. "You two head in, we'll stay back with the horses."

The two archers headed into the woods on the other side of the road. The big man and his tall companion stayed on the road. After a few minutes, they tethered the horses and sat down. The tall man carried a shield that he leaned against a tree. Randall got a look at the sigil that adorned the oaken shield. It was a yellow bear.

Without thinking, Randall stood and drew his blade. He was furious. After generations of simmering animosity, Bear Clan had finally crossed the line. What could have caused the fools to break the peace in such a way? At that moment, he didn't care. Once the king found out, he would send an army to restore the peace. By that time, Heston Hold could fall. Randall would not allow that.

Even though he was irate, Randall kept his head. He crept silently to the edge of the woods and hid behind another tree. Dragonwing said nothing, but was impressed with Randall's restraint. Hot blood had led many a good warrior to his doom. Instead of being controlled by his anger, Randall was using it to steel his nerves. Hard as it was, he decided to be patient.

A few minutes later, it paid off. The tall man came to the tree line to pee, just a few feet away. Randall jumped into the air and brought his sword hilt down with all his might. The dragon bone hit the man in the temple, knocking him unconscious. Then Randall turned to face the big man, who was already drawing his broadsword.

*

Bisley was a strong man. Bisley was a brave man. Even though he was not as skilled as knights were, Bisley was a peerless soldier. He had never been afraid to face a man in armed combat. His strength and girth provided all the confidence he needed. Now he was in unfamiliar territory. When the Raven Knight leaped from the shadows, Bisley was terrified.

It moved from shadow to shadow with the fluid grace of a bird in flight. For a moment Bisley was a child again, listening to his grandmother's tales of animal spirits and totems, of supernatural hybrids come to extract vengeance for some hateful deed. Surely this was the raven spirit, here to protect its clan.

Training won out over fear, and Bisley hefted his heavy broadsword. His enemy lashed out, and the force of Bisley's parry drove the raven's sword into the ground. With a fearsome back swing, Bisley struck an eviscerating blow to his opponent's abdomen.

The raven lurched back at the last moment, and the broadsword only drew sparks across his belly. The creature yanked its blade from the ground and lunged. Bisley tried to raise his heavy sword in time to parry, but the raven was just too fast. Blow after blow broke through his feeble defenses. He should have been dead six times over. With each blow, the raven turned its sword at the last second, hitting Bisley with the flat of the blade. Every strike hurt worse than a punch, but didn't bite his flesh.

The last hit was to his sword hand. The useless appendage dropped the heavy blade. Then he was on his back, with the Raven Knight's sword at his throat.

Many years later, Bisley would tell this story to his grandchildren without shame. There would not be many who could say that they faced the legendary Raven Knight, and lived.

*

Killing a man proved to be very different than killing a kobold. The little lizard-things were intruders, bent on destroying this world. The fat bear in front of him was just a man following orders, not a crazed thing that needed to be put down. Randall couldn't do it. His clan loyalty tugged at him, but the quest he was tasked with had given him a new perspective. Petty squabbles between clans meant nothing compared to the dangers that faced them all. He had to stop this conflict, not make it worse.

"Why are you doing this?" he asked, blade pressed against the other man's throat. "Why are you here?"

"They killed nine of our men," said Bisley. "They came with a message for Lord Kodiak, all peaceful like. Then killed our boys in their sleep. Even Sir Leston."

"Who?" Randall asked.

"Clan Raven. Lord Claypool sent them," said Bisley.

That couldn't be true. This man was a low-ranking soldier. He was only repeating rumors he had heard. Lord Claypool would never have ordered such a brazen assault. Randall had to find out what really happened.

He went to the horses, and found a length of rope in one of the saddlebags. After binding and gagging both soldiers, Randall went back into the forest.

10

A thin layer of navy blue clouds dulled the light of the crescent moon. Shadows blossomed everywhere, and Randall had no trouble slipping unseen up Blackfeather Hill. The Bear army was massed at the east gate, so he made his way to the west gate of Heston Hold. As Randall edged around the corner of the wall, he saw campfires and tents halfway down the hill. There were at least a hundred soldiers. It would have been foolish to expect Bear Clan to leave the back door unguarded.

The wall provided ample shadow for Randall to sneak undetected to the gate. Two bear soldiers dozed at their posts. The first guard was knocked further unconscious before the other stirred. The second guard barely laid hand upon hilt before he, too, was knocked out.

Randall rapped on the gate three times quickly, two slow ones, then thrice more.

"Fat chance, bear," said a voice on the other side. "Cawing at dawn, ebony streak."

"Lashing out with razor-sharp beak," responded Randall. He had memorized all the codes and passwords long ago.

There was a sound of metal bars being pushed, then an eerie creak. A secret door opened, just a crack, beside the gate. When the guard saw Randall, he opened the door wider and pulled him in.

Through his helm, Randall caught faint whiffs of pig and potato, of horse dung and human waste. Not a pleasant aroma, but it smelled like home. It didn't *feel* like home, though. There was a somber tension in the air. Grim-faced soldiers manned their posts along the wall, while other men were fletching arrows or sharpening swords.

"Take me to see Lord Claypool immediately," Randall said in his most authoritative voice. "Even if he is abed, I must speak with him. Now."

He decided to keep his raven helm on for the time being. It would make him seem intimidating and mysterious. If he took it off and was recognized as a squire, getting to see Lord Claypool would take much longer. He would be forced to explain himself to the Captain of the guard, and then to the knights. The delay could take hours. He might not even get an audience until tomorrow. One of the nastier soldiers might even try to steal Dragonwing. Randall dreaded the idea of fighting his own people, but he would if he had to. It was better to have them believe that he was a messenger, with words for Lord Claypool's ears only.

"Hold on," said the gate sergeant. "We can't let some stranger have an audience in time of war. You could be an assassin. Who are you under there?"

"I'm the one who made it through enemy lines to bring a message to our liege lord. You are the one who will be blamed if this news is delayed any longer. If Lord Claypool decides that you need to know my identity, I'm sure he will tell you. Send guards with me if you must. I am going now." With that, Randall started walking.

There was a tense moment when he wasn't sure if they were going to draw steel. His heart was hammering in his chest. Then four of the guards fell in step behind him. His bluff worked. His armor was that of a knight, and knights were treated with respect. Defying a knight could be a fatal mistake, and the gate sergeant's fear outweighed his sense.

"Oh!" Randall called over his shoulder, more confident now. "Have Sir Darwyn meet me in the audience chamber."

*

The audience chamber doubled as the feasting hall. It was a large room with thick wood pillars. Each wall had two large hearths. Torches hung on the pillars and along the walls. The chamber was empty, but arguing voices could be heard coming from the back room. Randall strode past the chamber guards and headed towards the council meeting room before they had a chance to question him.

He burst into the council room. The booming voices trickled off as every head turned to look at him.

"Well, well," said Lord Claypool. "What have we got here?"

"This is an outrage!" said a large bearded man. "How did you get in here?"

"Be silent, Lord Garthos," said Lord Claypool. "This is most interesting. A Raven Knight. Yet I am Lord of the ravens, and I do not know you as one of my knights. How can this be?"

One of Claypool's advisors, a white-haired Elder in a long robe, whispered into his ear.

"Ah, yes," said Claypool. "The legend of the raven spirit, come to help us in our hour of need. I believe the story involved the spirit re-animating one of our dead warriors to help us overcome adversity. I would love to believe that you are my dear nephew Edwood, come back from the dead. Alas, I am not a superstitious man. Also, you are too short to be him."

The council members chuckled at that. Randall saw movement behind him. It was Sir Darwyn entering the room. Randall was nervous again, but there was no turning back.

"I've seen their army," Randall began. "They outnumber us, but we have the advantage of defense. If we fight this out, both sides will be decimated."

"My point exactly!" interrupted a weasel-faced man dressed in expensive clothes. Randall knew the man, Penduss, a wealthy merchant. "We have to find a peace."

"The only way they'll give us peace is if we give them Sir Bean!" roared Sir Garthos. "We've gone over this. It's unacceptable!"

"Their honor requires it," said a man that Randall didn't recognize. His long moustache trembled as he spoke. "They will not leave us in peace without someone to take the fall."

"Perhaps there is another way," said Randall. "Allow me to speak to them in your name."

"Preposterous!" shouted Garthos. Claypool silenced him with a look.

"That would not be wise," said Lord Claypool. "You are a stranger to us."

"I am no stranger," Randall said, removing his great helm. "I am one of you."

Randall turned to face his mentor. Darwyn's narrowed eyes suddenly widened.

"Randall, my boy!" cried Sir Darwyn, embracing him roughly. "Thank the Warrior, you're alive!"

Flooded with emotion, Randall didn't care about the tear that streaked down his cheek. He hugged his mentor fiercely. The child inside him wanted to crumble and sob. The man he was becoming refused. Once he was composed, he turned back to the council.

Knowing that he was family, the council opened up to him. They told him how it had come to this. Randall was saddened to find out that it had all started with him. When he was found to be missing, the raven host stayed where it was as scouts followed the trail of the turkey thieves. The trail led to the bear encampment. The search took the better part of a day, and the bear host was long gone by this time.

Upon returning to Heston Hold, Sir Darwyn was called back to his district on urgent business. He tasked Sir Bean with investigating his squire's disappearance. Bean led fifteen men to the bear capitol, Salmon Creek, to present their findings to Lord Kodiak. They never got an audience.

The men were given a cottage and barn to bed down for the night. At the witching hour, they were set upon by thirty hooded soldiers. They fought their way out and escaped bear territory with six casualties. Randall wasn't surprised that this version differed greatly from the story told to the bear soldiers.

After that point, the council was divided. Some thought Lord Kodiak was in on the lie, had concocted it as an excuse to attack.

Others thought that he had been manipulated. After hearing Randall's story, it seemed likely that Sir Corben had orchestrated the whole thing. Corben was irate and embarrassed by his early defeat in the joust at Darwyn's hand. It was Corben's squire, Mutt, who stole the prize turkey and chased Randall over the cliff. He was an angry man with something to cover up.

Randall also told them about his quest, and his magic sword. The council looked at him as though he was crazy. One of Lord Claypool's advisors, an Elder standing behind him, whispered in his master's ear for a few long minutes.

"I am told that being chosen is a great honor," said Claypool as he walked around the table towards Randall. "Vedi says that your destiny lies far beyond the territorial squabbles of your tribe. I already forgot half of what he said, but I think I should trust you on this. My trust does not come without cost. Know that if you fail, it will mean war, and you will not be allowed to return to us."

"Even when I succeed," responded Randall, "I shall not return. As you said, my destiny lies far beyond this place."

Lord Claypool shook his hand, and then embraced him.

"I may be taken for a fool for trusting you," said Claypool, "but I sense something in you. Something great."

*

After the meeting, Randall found himself on the terrace, gazing at the stars. It was decided that he would ride out the front gate at first light. He needed to sleep, but didn't know where to go. Sir Darwyn approached, offering his wineskin.

"Last I saw you, you were but a boy," said Darwyn. "A mere month has passed, yet now I see a man before me."

Randall beamed with pride, and the two shared a silent moment. Darwyn insisted that Randall stay the night at his home, and Randall gratefully accepted. They finished the wineskin, talking of old times. Randall retired to the guest room.

"You did great today." Dragonwing's voice jarred Randall from his slumber.

"What the hell happened to you?" Randall whispered angrily. "I needed you today. You haven't shut up in weeks, and when I really needed you, you disappeared."

"You didn't need me at all," the sword responded. "Consider today a test. You passed. Know that whenever you truly need me, I will be there."

Another lie, but this one could be forgiven. Dragonwing had no way of knowing the cruel twist that fate had in store for the young raven.

11

The first rays of the new rising sun illuminated frost on the leafless trees. Randall rode through the front gates on Sir Darwyn's second best horse. He carried the white and yellow diplomat flag on a spear, and was ushered through the bear camp unhindered.

Lord Kodiak was seated on a throne in front of the largest tent. Flags behind him rippled in the stiff breeze. Randall dismounted and took to knee.

"Lord Kodiak," said Randall. "I come to beseech you on behalf of both our clans. If you proceed with this assault, both our houses will be greatly weakened, maybe even destroyed. As punishment for breaking treaty, the king will annex your territory and depose you. I bring a way out."

"All we ask is Sir Bean," said Lord Kodiak, "that is your way out, and naught else." He did not speak with conviction. The hot blood that allowed him to agree to such a foolish venture had long since cooled, and he clearly saw the corner he had painted himself into.

"My lord," said Randall, "You have been led astray by your own knight, Sir Corben."

Kodiak's attendants burst into uproar over that, chief among them Corben himself.

"The only way past this," continued Randall, "the only way to avoid our mutual destruction, is by trial of single combat. Each side picks a champion, both sides retain honor, no one gets annexed."

Kodiak let his people argue over that for a moment. He glared at Corben with eyes of steel. Clearly he had already suspected something.

"I have heard of you, Raven Knight," said Lord Kodiak. "You could have killed two of my men, but chose not to. You seem to be an honorable man. Who would your side choose as champion?"

"I will fight, my lord." Randall said.

"And you will fight Sir Corben," said Lord Kodiak, sneering at his dishonored knight.

Corben dare not argue, lest he sully his family honor as well as his own. Thus they met, the rising raven and the falling bear, upon the field of battle.

*

They faced each other across a clearing: Clan Raven in a half-circle behind Randall, Bear Clan in a half-circle behind Corben. The midday sun was bright, but offered little warmth. Soldiers around the perimeter of the field were calling to their champions, but Randall barely heard them. His attention was entirely focused on the knight in front of him.

Corben was tall and strongly built, clad in gleaming chain-and-plate armor. A thick oak shield was strapped to one arm, the other hand held a longsword. His eyes were grim under the steel half-helm he wore. They walked to within a few yards of each other, and then Corben charged.

Randall raised his borrowed shield to deflect the blow as he spun around. His back swing caught Corben on the armored nape of the neck. The big knight tumbled forward and landed on his face. A roar of laughter erupted from the Raven spectators. Randall allowed himself a little smile. This was like the tournament, when Sir Darwyn embarrassed Sir Corben in much the same way. This was going to be easy.

"Don't get cocky," said Dragonwing. "Just get in there and finish him quick."

It was too late for that. Sir Corben was already standing. His face was red, and spittle flew from his lips as he cursed and screamed. His eyes burned with fury. Clearly he was remembering his shame at the tournament as well.

Blind anger made a man forget his training, made him make stupid mistakes. Randall would let the man defeat himself. Corben swung his sword in a wide arc, which Randall easily parried. The big knight quickly swung his heavy shield from the other side. Randall didn't even see it coming.

Lights exploded in Randall's head as he sunk to one knee. His mouth was full of blood and bits of teeth. He couldn't think straight. The big shield slammed into his chest and suddenly Randall was on his back, gasping for air. A cold smile curled Corben's lips.

Randall weakly raised his own shield just in time to block a vicious swing from Corben's blade. Pain lanced up his arm from the impact. The big knight swung again and again. Randall didn't think his opponent would be so fast. Sir Corben was a trained knight, and Randall had foolishly underestimated him.

His shield started to crack under the onslaught. As Corben raised his sword for another strike, Randall rolled out of the way, dropping his broken shield. He lashed out with his sword, catching the back of Corben's leg. The big man fell to his knees and howled.

Randall tried to run, but ended up stumbling awkwardly. His wits were still scrambled from the headshot he took. He needed time to clear his head, time to think. He wouldn't get it. Corben was already rising.

Randall took a deep breath and tried to focus.

"Remember the kobolds," said Dragonwing.

What about the kobolds? Back in the cave, Dragonwing insisted that he learn their methods to use against them. That wouldn't work now. There was no time for observation; Corben was already coming at him. The big knight was stronger and better trained. Then it clicked. He had to *be* the kobold, had to attack in an unorthodox way that his opponent wouldn't suspect.

Sir Corben reared back for a crushing blow. Instead of dodging or trying to parry, Randall stepped close and kicked Corben's shield to the side. He jumped beside his foe, raking his blade across Corben's face. With his opponent momentarily distracted, Randall stabbed at Corben's shield arm. As the slab of oak hit the ground, Corben screamed in pain and rage.

Before Randall could think of another unexpected move, Corben was slashing again. The metallic sound of swords clashing filled the air as each man blocked, attacked, and then blocked again. Randall knew he couldn't go much longer. He parried a shot wide, and then quickly punched Corben's exposed face with a steel gauntlet. There was a loud crack as teeth and blood sprayed from Corben's mouth.

Randall stepped in for the killing blow, slashing at Corben's head. The big man blocked, and then stepped forward, slamming hard into Randall. Randall stumbled and fell onto his back. Corben thumped down onto him, trapping both swords between them. The big knight was too heavy. Randall saw blackness creeping in at the edge of his vision. If he couldn't escape, he would soon pass out. One of the blades was digging into his shoulder between the armor plates, cutting deep.

His free hand found the hilt of his dagger. As the darkness took him, Randall stabbed as hard as he could into Sir Corben's chest.

12

Even before he opened his eyes, he smelled it: A clean, soap smell. It had been weeks since his last bath, and he had gotten used to his own stench. Randall slowly stretched, enjoying the lightness and freedom of being out of that heavy armor. He wondered how long he was—

Out of his armor?

He sat bolt upright, eyes wide, fists coiled. He was alone in a small room, sitting on a cot. Randall tried to stand and tripped over the blanket wrapped around his legs. He landed with a thud on the stone floor. Now he was fully awake. He heard footsteps approaching. He looked around frantically, hoping to find some weapon to defend himself with.

"I'm right here, you nincompoop," said Dragonwing. Sure enough, the magic blade was lying on the floor right beside the cot. "You're safe. You won."

The door opened, and a comely middle-aged woman stepped in. "Darling," she called over her shoulder. "He's awake."

Sir Darwyn entered the room with a broad smile on his face.

"You did it, my boy," said Darwyn. "The bears have packed up, and they are leaving. Lord Claypool even went out to meet with Lord Kodiak. They shared a few private words, and then shook hands. Lord Kodiak seems an honorable man; I hope he can keep his men in check.

"Now — how do you feel?"

Randall thought about it. His mouth hurt the most. Probing with his tongue, he found a wadded bandage stuffed into a hole where one of his upper molars had been. There were a few other teeth with sharp edges where they had chipped. Next was the shoulder. The pain shot from the top of his arm, over the collarbone, and onto his chest. He looked down to see the whole area bandaged perfectly. Darwyn's wife had clearly done this many times before.

"I am fine," Randall lied, knowing that once the armor was back on, his pain would dull and the wounds would heal quicker. "Time is short, I must be on my way."

"First you will break your fast with us," said Sir Darwyn. "Then Lord Claypool would like to meet with you, before you set forth."

*

A light but steady snow was falling as they made their way across the courtyard. Randall wore his armor, and carried his gear with him. Darwyn had outfitted him with sacks of cheese, hard sausages, biscuits, a few pounds of salt beef, and skins of wine and water. Also some perishables: fruit, vegetables, and loaves of bread.

Darwyn also made gift of a suit of chain-and-plate armor, "in case you lose your sword, and the armor that comes with it!" Randall was happy to find that when he donned his raven armor atop the other armor, the weight and flexibility were like he was wearing only one. Dragonwing told him it was a good idea. All its previous bearers had done the same thing.

Unlike the last time he was here, Randall had to stop at the doorway to the audience chamber, so he could be announced. An octet of trumpets bleated an entrance theme. As they fell silent, a voice called out: "May I present Squire Randall Delaine, hero of Blackfeather Hill."

Randall entered to the sounds of applause and cheering. The hall was filled with people: noble houses in the front, lesser houses in the rear. The sound was deafening.

He walked the aisle alone, with many well-wishers patting him on the back and thanking him. He felt so light and free, for a minute he thought he must have been dreaming.

Lord Claypool was on a raised dais, sitting on his ornately carved ebony throne. Randall seemed to see everything for the first time. The screaming raven head carved from the chair back, the sharp talons jutting from the arm rests. He felt like time had slowed down. Every word spoken was weighed down with great importance. This was one of the defining moments of his life.

Lord Claypool was wearing his parade armor, complete with silver scabbard. He stood, then drew his blade and held it aloft.

"Kneel and bow," he said softly. Randall did.

"Let it be known," began Lord Claypool in a booming voice, "that Randall, son of Milos, squire of Sir Darwyn, is a hero this day.

Now and forevermore, each and every one of us owes him our gratitude. Lets raise a cheer for him."

The crowd erupted in a chorus of huzzahs. Randall felt so small, like a shrinking mote on the ocean of existence. Then his pride swelled and he felt big again.

Once the voices died down, Lord Claypool continued: "His deeds have earned our praise and esteem. His valor has earned something more."

Claypool placed his blade upon Randall's left shoulder. "You knelt as Squire Randall Delaine."

He moved the blade to Randall's right shoulder. "You rise as Sir Randall, the Raven Knight."

Randall stood. He knew without reservation that this was the happiest moment of his life, and he enjoyed every moment of it. Darwyn stood beside him, applauding loudly, with tears in his eyes. Trumpets blazed. People cheered. Randall absorbed it all.

It was only later, in the dark cold nights ahead, that he realized what that meant. He would never be this happy again. This was the last golden memory of his life *before*.

13

Four days out of Heston Hold the snow really started coming down. At least, it was four periods of asleep-and-awake. Everything was a blur of white and gray, who knew what was night or day anymore? Randall was headed east, as Dragonwing had advised. The snow was flying horizontally, stabbing into his left eye, and blinding it. He donned his helm, and the snow on his face quickly melted. He felt something pulling in his forehead, drawing him towards his goal.

"That is the compass," said Dragonwing. "It leads us in the direction of the prism. We can deviate for terrain or circumstance, but will always follow the general direction."

"So now I've got a magnet in my head," said Randall. "Fantastic! Could you put a fire in my chest so I don't freeze solid?"

That was one thing the Sword couldn't do. Cold was cold. On the other hand, the Sword's magic did extend to the horse.

"Do you declare this horse to be your loyal steed?" Dragonwing had asked on their first day out. "Is this the one?"

There was no question. He was the best horse that Randall had ever ridden, the first gift from Sir Darwyn. "Yes."

The horse *changed*. He seemed to become wider and taller. Black plate mail with feathered motif appeared on his chest and flanks. He could run almost twice as fast and required half as much food as he did before. Nightwind was his name.

Now, Nightwind was just a horse, trudging through a blizzard. Behind them trotted a pack mule that Randall had taken from Heston Hold. The mule carried a bedroll, a small tent, fresh clothes, and some other gear. The rations were divided between both animals' saddlebags. Large saddlebags carried only enough horse feed for a week of travel, so Randall would have to find food for them where he could.

A large white hump emerged from the flakes and shadows. Randall was glad to see it was an inn. Paying for lodgings and food wouldn't be a problem; Lord Claypool had given him enough coin to live comfortably for a year. Leaving Nightwind and the mule at the hostelry, Randall took a room until the storm blew out. Two days later, a foot and a half of snow greeted him when he set out.

Facing the blazing sunshine reflecting off the freshly fallen snow, Randall's thoughts were of darkness. On his first night out of Heston Hold, he couldn't sleep. He closed his eyes and saw Corben's dead eyes staring back at him. It hit him like a hammer to the chest: killing a human wasn't like killing a kobold. He emptied his stomach; hurling pulped orange and mashed sausage onto the snow. After the high of being named a knight, this low was devastating.

His mood was as dark as the sky. He had been raised, as all boys were, with tales of knights and warriors, of great battles and horrific monsters. All those stories were filled with death. The world was a savage place, with war and sickness and misery all around. Death had been a part of his life for as long as he could remember. Why did he feel so bad after killing a man, even one who was trying to kill *him*? How could he be a hero if killing a man caused him such pain and confusion?

"That is precisely *why* you can be a hero," Dragonwing said. "Because you understand the value of life."

"Stop reading my thoughts, sword!" Randall said angrily.

"Apologies," said Dragonwing. "When your emotions run high, your thoughts are too loud to ignore. You'll have to work on that. There are malevolent mind-mages out there who could use that against you."

"Right now I'm not worried about mages," said Randall. "I just want to forget this so I can get some sleep."

"Forgetting this feeling is the last thing you want," Dragonwing said. "You need to feel all of it, let it work through your system. Corben wont be the last man you ever kill. You need to know that next time it happens, you are stealing something sacred. If a man forgets that, he becomes a cold killer. That is not your way. If you don't have to kill someone, don't. Try to find another way to achieve your goal. On the other hand, if you do have to kill, don't hesitate. If there is no other option, you do what you have to do with no remorse. This is a delicate tightrope you must walk."

At the depths of his depression, those words made no sense to him. After relaxing for two days in the inn, when he emerged into that perfect white morning, he began to understand. Back in the cave, Dragonwing told him that he would be a knight and a hero.

Although he hadn't believed it at the time, the first part had come true. Randall was now a real knight. The Sword had proved itself wise in many ways; it only stood to reason that its prediction about Randall becoming a hero would come true as well. Back home they called him the hero of Blackfeather Hill, but he knew that didn't actually make him a hero. Becoming a knight required that he become more than the average man. To become a true hero, he knew that he had to always keep an essence of humanity and humility at his core. He had to cultivate a gentle and loving spirit, even in the face of whatever horrible adversities he may encounter. That was the tightrope that Dragonwing spoke of.

*

Nightwind's hooves were the first to break snow outside the stable. The horse sensed Randall's mood, and was eager to set out. Even with the mule slowing them down, they traveled many miles each day. Every night Randall would tie two thick sailcloths to some trees, on an angle, to act as wind block and roof for the animals. When he could find dry wood, he would make a fire. Other nights he would shiver in his little tent, rolled tightly in his bedroll.

One evening, as he was roasting a freshly caught hare on a spit above a roaring fire, he fell into a playful mood.

"Hey, sword!" The corners of Randall's mouth twitched up for a moment, the shadow of a smile.

"My name is Dragonwing."

"Yes."

"A sword is an inanimate implement. I am a legendary weapon."

"Of course you are."

Dragonwing recognized the game right away, and played along. "You *will* respect me, Human!"

Randall tried to keep a straight face, but couldn't. Although he had been walking like a man these last few days, his laughter was that of a boy, high and pure. The Sword joined in with its curious metallic chuckle.

Later, after the hare was mostly devoured, Randall got to thinking about the future.

"What happens after this quest is over?" he asked. "What happens if we win?"

"Not if. *When.*" Dragonwing said. "Our success is not in question, don't forget that. After our quest is done, you can return to your life. Claim your lands, take a wife, sire some children, whatever you like. Some of my bearers lived to a ripe old age, others died in war, or from disease."

"And what of you?" asked Randall. "Do you just disappear?"

"In a sense, I suppose," said Dragonwing. "For a while, at least. My physical body, the sword, if you will, remains. But my enchantments, the armor, my very self: all gone. I don't know what happens. I call it the great sleep, but it isn't the same as when you sleep. I'm just not here. As soon as you touch my blade to the prism, my enchantments will deactivate it. Then the magical feedback will cast me out. In the past I have been gone as little as a few hours and as much as a few days."

"Then what, you wait for the next one?" Randall asked.

"No. The bond is for life. I stay with my knights until they die, and I'm usually buried with them."

"The bond is for life?" Randall asked with a laugh. "So I'm stuck with you until I die? What happens if there's another emergency when I'm an old man?"

"That has happened only once. The odds are in your favor."

"I sure feel lucky. What happened to the one?"

"Sir Borrik was seven-and-fifty when his second portal opened," said Dragonwing. "He died valiantly as he closed it."

"Well," said Randall with a smile, "at least I have something to look forward to."

14

A week later they came to a river. Ice had formed at its edges, but the water was moving too swiftly to freeze over. The river was thirty feet wide, and too deep to cross. Randall decided to travel along the riverbank until he found a safer spot to ford. It took longer to meander along the curving river than it would to go straight, but he didn't mind. The water would attract thirsty animals. Sure enough, the next morning he spied a young boar, and felled it with an arrow. He spent a few hours cleaning, gutting, and preparing the carcass. That night he would feast on ham steak, the next morning on bacon.

When the sun reached its zenith, Randall still had the taste of bacon on his lips. He was lost in thought when he heard a scream and a splash from around the river bend. He kicked Nightwind to a gallop, dropping the mule's rope so he could get a good speed. The horse dodged trees and jumped over snowy logs effortlessly.

The river was narrower here, perhaps fifteen feet across. On the other side was a wagon with its front wheels in the water. The horse that had been pulling it was thrashing in the water, unable to stand.

"Broken leg," said Dragonwing.

"He's going to drag the whole wagon in," Randall said, sliding down from the saddle. He quickly tied Nightwind's reins to a tree, and then waded into the water. Even through his armor's enchantments, the water was so cold it stole his breath for a moment.

Across the water, a small old robed man was scrambling down the front of the wagon, into the water. He was trying to cut through the thick ropes that tied horse to wagon. His small knife hadn't gotten through one rope before Randall reached him.

"Back off, I've got it," said Randall, unsheathing his sword. The horse was still thrashing, and the wagon rolled further into the river. Randall sliced with all his might, cutting all four ropes at once.

The horse was swept away in the current. Randall turned to the old man, to offer a hand out of the water. The old man reached forward, then his eyes widened and his mouth formed a surprised

'O' as he lost his footing. In a blink, the old man was underwater, following the horse downstream.

Randall threw Dragonwing at the wagon, and then he dove into the river. The cold was staggering, but he willed his limbs to move. In any other suit of armor, he would have sunk like a stone. In this armor, he swam like a fish. He grasped at every shadow, finding only rocks and branches. Finally, when his lungs were burning and he could hold his breath no longer, his hand grasped an ankle.

Randall rose from the water, out of breath and shivering, with the small man in his arms. He collapsed on the riverbank. Randall was soaked, and his hands and feet were so cold they felt like they were on fire. He rolled over with a great effort, and tried to shake the old man awake. No response. Ravens were not a water people, but Randall had learned to swim as a child. He had seen a boy nearly drown once, and knew what to do. He pushed down on the old man's chest a few times, then bent down to breathe into his mouth. The old man coughed water into his face. Randall sat back to wipe his face as the old man emptied a surprising amount of river water into the snow.

Once he regained his composure, the old man turned to Randall. "Thank you, my friend. You saved my life."

"It wont mean a thing if we freeze to death here," said Randall. "We'd best be headed back. We need to start a fire. A big one."

"Agreed," said the man, smiling broadly. He held out his hand, and Randall shook it. "My name is Raxus, and I am in your debt."

"I am Randall, they call me the Raven Knight. Come now," he said, pulling Raxus to his feet. "Lets move, before we can't."

It took nearly an hour, but they made it back. The wagon was still there, it hadn't moved. They decided to leave it where it was; making a fire was the first priority. Across the river, Nightwind was still tethered to the tree. The mule was there as well. The animals had been digging snow while they waited, and both were nibbling on frozen grass.

Randall went to gather firewood, while Raxus rummaged in the back of his wagon.

"Ah, here we go," said the old man at last. "Come, boy. This will warm us better than any fire."

Randall came back to the wagon and dropped his armload of wood. Raxus was holding out a glass bottle with red liquid inside. Expecting rum or some other alcohol, Randall took a sip. It was no alcohol. It tasted like spices and fire. He coughed furiously and handed the bottle back. With each cough, he felt heat radiate from his belly, flowing out along his arms and legs. When normal breath returned, he felt warmer than he had in days. Looking down, he saw that the snow around his feet was melting.

"What is this? Some kind if witchcraft?" Randall asked.

"No, this is better," said Raxus. "I have studied the natural sciences; learned of reactions produced by certain elements, minerals, or plants. I have studied ancient Elven magics. The blending of these two fields is called alchemy. This is my trade, I am an alchemist."

"That's fascinating," said Dragonwing in a testy tone. "Now that you're all warm and cozy, feel free to retrieve me at your convenience."

The Sword was wedged in the fork of a tree. Randall chuckled as he placed his leg against the tree for leverage and pried the blade from its awkward position.

"Most of my wares are too expensive for the common folk," Raxus said. "Obtaining ingredients, performing rituals, these things are costly. Sometimes I will trade with wizard or shaman for spell or totem. Mostly I sell to princes and kings, lords and barons. Since I am in your debt, I offer you the pick of my wares. Things you could never afford to buy, whatever you want."

"How about that concoction we just drank?" Randall said. Even though he was warm, he busied himself by making a fire. "That would make my winter journey much easier if I could drink my warmth every night. I'll take a bottle of that."

"The Magma is for emergencies only," said Raxus. "If you drank it twice in one week, it would burn you alive from the inside."

"If all your potions have such a downside," said Randall, as spark took to flame, "then perhaps I would be better off without."

"We shall see," said Raxus, with a twinkle in his eye.

15

It took some coaxing, but Randall managed to get Nightwind and the mule across the frigid river. Raxus dried the animals off as Randall fried bacon. It wasn't truly bacon, since it hadn't been cured; it was only strips of fresh boar. After breakfast was done, they tied horse and mule to the back of the wagon, and pulled it out of the water.

Raxus had come from the east, and knew of a town four days away where he could get a new horse. Randall offered to let his animals tow the wagon that far. As they traveled, Raxus told stories, each more outlandish than the last: He traveled far to the northern mountains to find an ice lotus. The flower grew in the territory of a fierce snow basilisk, and the alchemist narrowly escaped being turned into an ice sculpture. Another time he had been summoned by a harbor baron to help a barren wife bear children. The baron didn't follow the directions for administering the potion properly. Last Raxus heard, the baron had thirty-seven heirs. Another time, across the Haunted Sea, Raxus was on a quest to harvest the venom of a certain fearsome asp. The Pharaoh of Hawk Clan demanded some of the venom to finish off his troublesome brother. Raxus was only halfway through his ritual when the Pharaoh's guards stole the potion. They snuck the unfinished potion into the brother's food. He mutated into a strange snake-man hybrid, and killed the Pharaoh and his court.

Randall didn't know whether to believe the stories or not, but he found himself liking Raxus. The little man was wise, and had seen much.

On their second day together, after lunch, Raxus was in the middle of one of his tales. Prince Rathashan of Tiger Clan asked to light up the sky on a special night with his mistress. The prince left the powders in his pocket. During the frolicking, the fire powders ignited. The cottage burnt up, and so did his clothes. The prince had to return to the palace with leaves covering his privates.

Randall was swaying back with laughter when the arrow struck the side of his neck. He had forgotten to don his helm after finishing lunch. He fell from the wagon, grasping at the arrow stuck in his flesh. *Some magic armor,* he thought, as his face smashed into the snow.

Nightwind and the mule reared to a halt. Fifteen fur-clad barbarians emerged from the trees. Randall stood on shaky legs and drew Dragonwing. Since he was still alive, the arrow must not have hit anything vital, but the pain was intense. He stumbled toward the wagon just in time to avoid another arrow. The blood flowing down his chest made it hard to concentrate. The barbarians were still twenty feet away, too far to strike at. Randall decided to go for his quiver, which was still slung on Nightwind. Peeking around the corner of the wagon, he saw Raxus slip down the other side and dash into the trees. He was just a coward after all, despite all his stories.

Randall ran to Nightwind, retrieved his quiver, and then ran back behind the wagon. The bow of Kolara formed in his hand, and he tried to fire. The pain in his neck made his arm shake, and his first shot went awry. On his second shot he held his breath to lessen his shaking, and compensated for the wind. The arrow struck true. The first archer was down. Randall was aiming for the second archer when some movement caught his eye. A barbarian emerged from the trees to rejoin his tribe. He dropped something that looked like a stone, and then walked back into the woods. Randall fired his bow, taking out the last archer. The barbarians started to charge. Then came the explosion.

A concussive bang knocked Randall to the ground, scattering the bow and arrows. An orange fireball engulfed most of the barbarians. Three survivors turned and ran once they saw what had become of their brothers. One confused soul ran straight at Randall, blade drawn. Dragonwing cut him down.

Another barbarian emerged from the woods. Randall turned, sword at the ready. The man was unarmed. His image flickered, and then suddenly it was Raxus standing there.

Randall couldn't make any sense of it. He was feeling light-headed and dizzy, and all he wanted to do was lay down. He fell to his knees, gaping uncomprehendingly at the red droplets in the snow beneath him. He looked at the arrow protruding from his neck, laughed once, and then fell over.

*

He had a faint memory of screaming as the arrow was pulled out, and then he woke in a dim tent. The tent was of a strange design, with fur around the doorway. It smelled of barbarian sweat, but at least it was warm.

Randall checked his neck wound. The bandage was primitive, but it would serve. The pain seemed to be gone. He tried moving his arm. It hurt, but not nearly as much as it should have. He likely had one of the alchemist's potions to thank for that.

The tent flap opened and Raxus entered with a gust of wind and snow. The old man handed Randall a bowl of stew.

"Eat up, my friend," said Raxus. "Our attackers may have been ill-tempered and ill-smelling, but they did leave us some welcome gifts. I found two of their horses, laden with this tent and some food."

"Thank you," said Randall, taking a bite. "For the stew, and for fixing up my wound as well. I guess this makes us even."

"My life for your bandaged neck?" Raxus said, bemused. "I hardly think we are even. I am still in your debt. We will go through my wares, I'm sure we'll find a few items that you will find useful. I've got Oil of Ingress; just one drop and any lock or door will be open to you. I've got Dreamroot Tea; a cup before bed will give you prophetic dreams. I've got—"

"Hold on," interrupted Randall. "How did you heal my wound?"

"I wrapped it in a herbal poultice," said the alchemist, "and fed you a few drops of Healing Water."

"Healing Water," said Randall. "I'll definitely need some of that."

"As you wish."

"Another thing," said Randall, setting aside the empty bowl. "What happened earlier? Are you some kind of shape-shifter?"

"No, no," laughed Raxus. "That's called `Feddik's Balm of Lesser Disguise'. It lets you take the appearance of anyone you see, clothes and all. It works best in a large crowd, where no one will notice two identical people. We got lucky; those barbarians were too stupid to notice me. The effect lasts only a few minutes, ten at most."

"I'd like one of those, as well."

"As you wish."

"By any chance, did Feddik invent a balm of greater disguise?"

"Oh yes," answered Raxus. "But I would never make that. Too many side effects."

"I see," said Randall, lost in thought. "What about that explosion?"

"Well, here we are then," tittered Raxus. "You've meandered your way to what you really wanted to know. What about that explosion? Indeed. That was a small Boom-bag. I also have large ones. There is but one side effect. If you do not follow my directions to the letter, you *will* blow up."

"I understand," said Randall. "Give me five of the large ones, and we are even."

"As you wish."

16

It was their last night together. Raxus decided to take the two barbarian horses and head west. Randall had to continue east, to wherever that strange magnetic tug in his head bade him. Raxus offered to show Randall his map.

"Look here," he said, unrolling a blank scroll. "These are the lands as I have seen them, from here to the Eastern Sea."

As Raxus waved his hand over the scroll, details appeared: mountains and rivers, forests and towns.

"Memorize this," Dragonwing whispered.

Randall needed to orient himself. He pushed through the tent flap into the crisp night. It was cold and cloudless. He looked to the stars. The Archer's bow was the easiest constellation to find. His bow was aimed at The Temptress. Her arms pointed up to the Raven's Eye. Each Clan had its own name for the North Star; Randall knew it as the Raven's Eye. Once he knew where true north was, he turned the map to orient it. Then he closed his eyes, feeling the strange tug in his forehead. He laid his hand across the scroll.

"This is where I must go," said Randall, opening his eyes. The route his hand traced went through the Spiderwept woods, into the Titantooth Mountains.

"Why does that seem familiar?" asked Dragonwing, in a small voice.

"That is ill news, my friend," said Raxus, shaking his head. "Your way will be harsh and troubled."

*

They left the next morning, but not until Raxus had spent an hour giving precise directions for using his alchemical concoctions. The old man led Randall a ways from the wagon before he gave the instructions for using the Boom-bags. He didn't want to accidentally detonate any while discussing the activation passwords. Since he knew that Randall could read, he even gave him piece of bark with the passwords carved into it. Once Raxus was sure that Randall could pronounce the words properly, they parted.

Two days later, Randall came to a road, just where the map said it would be. The going was a little easier since other hooves had already flattened the snow. The road led him to a small town where he replenished his supplies, and spent the night. After five more days of travel he came to another town, the last one he would see before entering the forest. Webury was the seat of Spider Clan, a small house that Randall knew nothing about. There was no castle, just a crumbling fort in the middle of town. All the buildings were old and sagging. The town had a bleak, unwelcome feel to it. Randall decided to stop only long enough to buy some more food. He made camp past the town, at the edge of the Spiderwept woods.

At dawn he entered the dense forest. There was no road, just a narrow path. A mixture of oak and pine at the outskirts soon gave way to the great cedars that dominated this part of the woods. Their limbs jutted out at odd angles, forming eerie shadows.

"Those shadows look a lot like spider legs," said Randall. "That must be where the forest got its name."

"Let us hope that is true," said Dragonwing.

It wasn't true at all.

The third night in the forest, as Randall was building a fire, a movement in the trees caught his eye. He retrieved his bow, watching intently. He had seen no game since entering the forest, and didn't want to miss his chance. The creature moved again, momentarily reflecting firelight at him. Hoping the reflection was a rabbit's eye-shine, Randall was disappointed to see it was just a spider. The thing looked shiny, as though it were made of ice. Its legs clicked softly as it walked up a tree trunk. The spider was about the size of his hand.

"Well, I'm not going to eat that thing," said Randall.

As he tied the quiver back on to Nightwind's saddlebag, he heard more clicking from above. Another spider fell from the darkness and landed on the mule's rear. The animal brayed with surprise. Randall quickly knocked the spider to the ground, and crushed it with his boot. The clicking sounds were all around him. Randall grabbed the mule's rope, and walked towards Nightwind.

Then came the spiders.

From all sides they came, at least fifty of them. The mule cried out as it was bitten. More spiders dropped from above, descending on their gossamer threads. Randall jumped into the saddle, swatting away spiders from his horse and himself. He started to pull the mule, but it was no good. The poor animal was thrashing, trying to get away from the spiders that swarmed its back and legs. Randall had no choice; he had to let go of the rope. The mule fell over as the spiders overtook it.

Nightwind was terrified. The horse reared up on its hind legs. A large shape emerged from the shadows: a spider as tall as a man. Randall dug his heels in, urging the horse to a full run. He knocked off the last few spiders as he went. From behind came one final shriek from the mule, as the giant spider sunk its fangs in.

After that, he decided to travel at night, and sleep in the day. One night he saw two of the giant spiders dancing in circles, some kind of mating ritual. The rest of the forest journey was uneventful.

A week later he emerged from the trees. He had lost his mule, his tent, and half of his food, but he was still alive. He still had his sword, and he still had his quest.

17

The wind was harsh as they entered the foothills. It whistled softly from the mountains ahead. Nightwind was moving slower now. Without the trees to block the wind, the winter seemed much bleaker. The bright white hope of new-fallen snow had faded to the dull gray of mid-winter despair.

The Titantooth Mountains loomed high and sharp up ahead. Their jagged peaks seemed to carve the sky above.

"This seems familiar," said Dragonwing. "Like I've been here before."

"You have traveled these lands?" asked Randall. "Why didn't you speak of this earlier? You talk about the value of fore-knowledge, but didn't tell me this?"

"It's not like that," said Dragonwing. "I wasn't really here, it was—I think it was a dream. I'm not used to this, it's so hard to remember. My mind isn't like yours, when I want to recall something, it comes right away."

"Dreams don't work like that, sword." Randall said. "Some things are true, some things are symbols, and some things are nonsense. You can't try to make sense of them with waking logic."

"I think the dream happened in my last great sleep, before I found you," said Dragonwing. "It comes in flashes. I remember these mountains. I remember the kobolds. I remember flying through the air, then intense pain, and then nothing. I didn't tell you before because it makes no sense."

"No, it doesn't," admitted Randall. "Maybe it was just a nonsense dream after all." That didn't feel right, but he didn't know what else to say.

The scrubland of the foothills was harsh. No game to be found, and hardly any grasses for Nightwind to dig up. Randall was forced to ration their food more severely. By now he had experienced traveling hungry. It was difficult, but necessary. He knew that he had to keep enough food stashed away so that he could be at full strength when he found the prism. He had no way of knowing what could be guarding the portal. It could be mad cultists, or ferocious monsters, or a sly wizard. It could be all of those, or maybe something completely different.

"I know that you don't know who or what I will face," said Randall. It was their second day in the foothills. The mountains loomed just ahead, an armory of snow-covered daggers. "You've told me about many kinds of monsters, but I don't think that will be the main problem. The portal will be opened by some kind of magic-user. Whether that means a cleric, a sorcerer, or a necromancer, I have no defense. Against sword, staff, or tooth, I know what to do. Dodge, parry, block, and attack. That makes sense to me. How do I dodge a spell? How do I block an incantation?"

"Just do what you do," replied Dragonwing. "I can disperse many spells as they manifest. Many others present a visual focus, something you can strike to diffuse the magic. If you were just some guy with some sword, you wouldn't stand a chance. We haven't fully explored everything that I can do. I was forged with one hundred and nineteen layers of enchantment. I can help defend you against magic."

Randall rode in silence for a few minutes, lost in thought. Then he chuckled, as he finally stumbled upon the right question. "We haven't fully explored what you can do. How many of these 'layers of enchantment' are devoted to defending against magic?"

"Ninety-six, I believe." If swords had mouths, Dragonwing would have surely been smiling. He always cherished the moment when a worthy bearer finally worked their way to the last question. That mingled feeling of wonder and foreboding when they learned the answer. Randall was almost there.

"That leaves twenty-three layers," said the Raven Knight. "If we include one for your great sleep, one for the armor, for the horse, the bow, the healing, the compass, for whatever else you have shown me, that still leaves a lot of enchantment. What have you not told me? What else can you do?"

There it was. Why did it always take the best ones so long to come to that question?

"What else can I do?" repeated Dragonwing, with a smile in his voice. "It is called 'The Metamorphosis'. It takes a lot of power, and I only have so much. So I can't do it often, and I can't do it for long."

"That sounds fantastically useless," said Randall. "What does it do?"

"Useless!" Dragonwing laughed in his odd, metallic way. "Not quite. In my first adventure, when Sir Llarys was facing the hordes of Thulos, do you think he just jumped headlong into the fray? Do you think that he was the bravest man who ever lived? Well, maybe he was, but he wasn't stupid. He knew there was no way that he would be able to fight his way through all of the harpies and demons that poured through the portal. He asked what else I could do. So I showed him. I turned him into a silver dragon. He flew over the demons, raining fire upon them. He landed at the portal, and then changed back into a man. He still had to do the last part himself, fighting bravely past harpies and the wizard, to lay my blade upon the prism. I used that power on many of the elves, transforming them momentarily into dragons, but only the ones who asked. Once, across the Eastern Sea, I used 'Metamorphosis' on Quan Tse-Tao. I turned him into a giant praying mantis so he could sneak through the jungle, above his enemy's heads."

"So you're saying this 'Morfus' will transform your bearer into the symbol of his house?" asked Randall. "You can change me into a raven? Why didn't you do this before? You could have saved us a lot of travel time."

"It doesn't work that way," said Dragonwing. "You had to be ready, you had to ask for it. Besides, it only works for a short period of time. We would have only shaved a few days off our journey, maybe a week. It drains me, and it will hurt you, so we cant do it often."

"Alright," said Randall. "When will we use this power?"

"When we have no other choice," Dragonwing sighed.

18

Steel-gray sky pressed down from above. Sharp rocks and shadowed snow pulled from below. Four days into the mountains, Randall walked with Nightwind in tow. They were on a precariously narrow trail. Sheer rock wall on the left, terrifying drop to the right. The wind was fickle; one moment calm, the next moment so strong that it threatened to pull him right off the mountain. He hugged the rock wall with one hand and tried to calm Nightwind with the other.

The cold was worse than he had ever felt. His fingers and toes were numb. When the wind came, it cut through his cloak and two layers of armor as though he were naked. He found himself dreaming of a sip of Magma, the warming potion from that alchemist. It was a good thing that Raxus hadn't given him any. After facing this cold, Randall would have surely drunk more than twice in one week, gladly burning alive from the inside.

Hunger seemed to make the cold even worse. Nearly starving, he had still managed to save enough for one good meal. He knew he wouldn't have to wait long. The compass was buzzing so ferociously in his forehead, he had to ask Dragonwing to turn it off. Once they turned the last corner on the path, he understood why.

In a clearing in the wooded valley below, a glittering disk illuminated the twilight.

"The portal!" whispered Dragonwing. "We've made it!"

They hadn't quite made it. The pathway was still narrow, and the wind was still bitter. Twice, Randall thought that Nightwind would be blown off. The stubborn black warhorse pushed on through both times.

The path gradually leveled off and widened. Randall found the entrance to a cave hidden behind a large boulder. After carefully checking to make sure no bears or cougars were in residence, he led Nightwind inside.

The cave was warmer than he thought it would be. It was dark, but after spending nearly a month underground, Randall knew his eyes would adjust. He counted one hundred paces, decided that was enough, and settled down for the night.

After sleeping for a few hours, Randall was nudged awake by Nightwind. The horse had never been inside a cave, waking up in one seemed to have spooked it. Randall tried to calm Nightwind as they made their way back to the cave entrance. Once they could smell the fresh air coming from outside, the horse started to relax.

"You'd better eat now," said Dragonwing. "You may not get another chance."

Randall and Nightwind ate the last of their food.

"Don't worry," said Dragonwing. "Whoever we have to face must eat as well. You can steal some food from them."

"Oh sure," Randall said. "While I'm trying to save the kingdom, and trying not to get killed, I'll just pop over to the nearest cooking fire and ask what's for lunch."

"If your skills are as sharp as your wit," chuckled Dragonwing, "we may be doomed after all."

Outside the cave, the sky was still dark. Randall wove his way between boulders, the remnants of an avalanche. They rode downhill for an hour, into the valley. The sun slowly rose, blue gradually overtaking black. The valley was quite narrow, and heavily wooded. The going was steep. Across the valley was another mountain; its side was a sheer cliff that rose two hundred feet above the trees. Randall was glad that he didn't have to climb down on that side.

Some of these trees grew to well over a hundred feet tall, so he wasn't able to see the clearing or the portal. That didn't matter; he would see them soon enough.

"So, any last words of wisdom?" asked Randall. "Any final tricks up your sleeve? Or up your scabbard, I suppose."

"No tricks." Dragonwing said. "You know what to do. Try not to be seen for as long as you can. Make your way to the prism. It will be close to the portal, emanating the magic beam that keeps the portal open. Touch my blade to the prism, and it will sleep, closing the portal. Remember that I will sleep as well. I may be gone for a few hours, or a few days. Just use your wits, and try to stay alive."

"Try to stay alive," repeated Randall. "With a detailed strategy like that, how can we lose?"

"Every time I have done this, it has been completely different than all the others. There is no point planning before we know what we face." Dragonwing was serious, ignoring Randall's attempt at humor.

"Alright then," said the Raven Knight. "Let's find out what we're up against."

*

In the thick of the evergreen woods, the only sound came from Nightwind's hooves as they crunched through snow and twigs. Soon muffled sounds were coming from up ahead. As Randall rode closer to the clearing, the sounds gradually became muted voices and grunts. Many voices.

Randall dismounted and quietly walked to the tree line. He crouched down low. Slowly parting the branches of a small pine tree, he peered into the clearing.

Kobolds. A lot of them.

Some were eating, some were laughing, and some were fighting. There must have been at least eighty of the little lizard-men. Randall had faced a handful of them and emerged victorious, but this was too many. An open assault was out of the question.

"I only see kobolds," whispered Randall. "Could they have done this on their own? I can easily defeat one of their wee shaman if that's all it takes."

"Look to the portal," said Dragonwing.

The glowing disc was mostly blocked by pine needles, so Randall crawled to the other side of the tree for a better look. He gasped in surprise.

The portal was enormous, at least fifty feet tall. It was a thin, silvery luminescent disc that radiated a rainbow of light. It was beautiful. As he watched, twenty more kobolds emerged. The portal rippled like water as they stepped through.

"I had no idea it would be this big," whispered Randall. "I thought it would be a little taller than me. This is amazing."

"I have never seen a portal this large," admitted Dragonwing. "I didn't think this was possible."

"You said every time is different," whispered Randall. "Lets just close it quickly instead of worrying about its size. I don't see the prism, it must be behind the portal."

Dragonwing said nothing.

Randall crept back into the forest, walked stealthily until he was sure he had passed the portal, and then returned to the tree line.

The portal looked the same from the back. There were no kobolds on this side. There was no prism, either.

"Where is it?" Randall hissed. "You said there would be a prism. How am I supposed to close this thing now?"

"Calm yourself!" Dragonwing said in a stern tone. "I knew this one wasn't going to be easy. It is as I feared, the prism is on the other side."

"The other side of what?"

"Usually," said Dragonwing, "the Prism manifests on this world. A human mage opens the portal to let the enemy through. Sometimes, though, it will appear on another world. When that happens, a Greater Demon can open the portal without the aid of a human minion. That makes the situation much more dangerous. I thought I told you about all of this."

"Maybe you did." Randall was afraid. He had no idea what may be waiting for him on the other side of the portal. Now that he was here, so close to the end, it all seemed much too big for him. "Maybe I didn't think it would come to this. Can we go through the back of the portal, where there are no kobolds?"

"I'm afraid it doesn't work like that," replied Dragonwing.

"Well, there's no way that I can fight my way through the kobolds. I can't do this alone."

"First of all," said Dragonwing, "you aren't going to fight these kobolds. Second, you are not alone. Never forget that."

It was true. He wasn't alone. He tried to calm himself, breathing deeply. The time for childish fears was done. "How can we get past them without fighting?" asked Randall. "Should I use that potion from the alchemist to transform myself into a kobold, and just walk right through?"

"No, we're not going to walk through," said Dragonwing, with a smile in his voice. "We're going to fly."

19

The wind flowed smoothly across the clearing, no gusts. Perfect for takeoff. Randall walked into the clearing, with Nightwind trailing behind.

"Fly? You're sure that's the best way?"

"Absolutely," said Dragonwing. "With a portal this large, flying is the best option. If you go on foot, even temporarily disguised as a Kobold, who knows what you'll be walking into. In the air, we can fly forty feet above the heads of our enemies. We can study the situation. Take note of enemy positions, the lay of the land, and the location of the prism. We'll land well past the danger, and formulate a plan of attack."

"That makes sense." Randall glanced uneasily towards the mass of kobolds to his right. He felt exposed and vulnerable without the trees to hide him. If one of the kobolds happened to look in this direction, there would be no escape. "Lets do it now, while we still can."

"All right, lets begin," Dragonwing said eagerly. "When the change is done, you will feel a presence, another mind surrounding yours. That will be the raven mind. You don't know how to fly, but the raven does. Trust in the raven."

"I have no idea what that means," said Randall. He looked back at his horse, suddenly anxious. "What about Nightwind? I can't leave him here to be slaughtered by those monsters."

"You chose Nightwind as your loyal steed," said Dragonwing. "That means he is included in my enchantments. It is not only your body that makes the change. The total mass of you, your horse, and your gear determines the size of the raven you will become. This is going to be one large bird."

The sounds from the Kobold camp had faded to the back of Randall's mind, until the voices changed. Cries of alarm were the same in any language. He turned his head to see the nearest monsters begin to charge.

"NO!" cried Randall. "Go, go, go! Get this Morfus spell going!"

"Metamorphosis," corrected Dragonwing. "It has already begun. Embrace your horse."

Randall grabbed hold of Nightwind's neck. Every hair on the horse's mane seemed so clearly defined. The hair between his fingers, so close, until he was inside. Blood flowing like a raging river with each beat of the horse's heart. Of the man's heart. Of another's heart.

Sky and tree blurred and swirled. Sound stretched out and folded in upon itself. Sensation overwhelmed until, for a moment, he could feel nothing at all.

Then he was bird.

*

Raven bent its neck to nibble at a wing. The feathers had to be properly primped and groomed before it could fly. The little orange screamers were getting closer, but they seemed so insignificant. Right wing ready, Raven started on the left. The nearest orange screamer threw its spear. The spear stung like a bee, then fell to the snow. Just a few more nibbles. The left wing was ready, and then the kobolds were upon him.

Anger! Raven lashed out with its beak, devouring two of the screamers heads. The knight inside struck out with razor talon, killing two more. The screamers stopped their charge, giving Raven a wide berth.

Raven ran into the wind, wings spread. The knight inside caused it to stumble, still unsure of this new form. *Trust the Raven.* The knight withdrew, and Raven flapped its wings.

The knight inside couldn't resist; he had to take control. Takeoff was the most crucial time. He twitched a wing at the wrong moment, the sky spun, and then Raven was rolling in the snow.

Raven stood quickly, shaking snow off its feathers. The screaming kobolds resumed their charge.

"You must let go." The sword inside sounded so far away.

The knight let go.

Raven took flight. It was so quick. Wing caught crosswind, and up Raven went. In a moment, the kobolds were as small as ants. With a twenty-foot wingspan, the giant Raven circled the sky.

The sword inside suggested flying into the silver. Raven agreed.

The huge bird swooped down into the portal.

*

Then it stopped in mid-air. Not frozen, for it was no longer cold. Time slowed. Thought slowed. It was like swimming through gelatin.

All was white and blue from snow and sky. A moment of violet. Then red. Then heat.

A pop as body emerged from gelatin.

A brief dive before recovering. A flurry of feathers, then flight.

*

As blur coalesced into vision, shadow was everywhere. Raven flew higher. What could be big enough to cast such a shadow?

A quick whistle of air, then two knuckles from a giant hand swatted Raven like a bug.

Spinning, spinning, then trees and branches, then dirt and stop. The Raven was done.

20

Randall found himself on the ground, with his face pressed up against Nightwind's brow. The pain nearly knocked him unconscious again. Sharp feathers were withdrawing into his every pore, digging like hungry razors. The horse sprung to its feet, ready for action.

Everything was red. The ground was scarlet rust, the trees were contorted crimson horrors. The heat took his breath away, and flattened him to the ground. Past the canopy of skeletal trees, twin suns blazed down.

"Snap out of it!" Dragonwing cried. "We've got to go!"

Randall shook his head side to side. The air was too thick to breathe. He just wanted to sleep. Nightwind nudged him and nibbled at his fingers.

"Okay, okay," mumbled Randall, slowly climbing into the saddle. "I'm awake."

The horse trotted into the woods, half-unconscious rider slumped on its back.

Randall woke to the sound of a drinking horse. They were beside a narrow creek. Strange six-winged bugs hovered overhead. His skin itched and his head throbbed. He rolled off the horse and dipped his head into the creek, drinking deeply. The water was warm, but pure.

"Well, that was strange," said Randall. He had regained his wits, and was once more seated on Nightwind. "I see why you don't do that Morfus thing often. If I never turn into a raven again, that'll be fine with me."

"You flew, and you are alive," said Dragonwing. "If you walked through, you might be dead now."

"There's that," said Randall, "so I suppose it wasn't all bad."

"Now we must hurry," said Dragonwing. "Every moment we waste, more kobolds could be crossing through to our world. Stay hidden in the trees, but ride back to the portal as fast as you can."

The ride was quick. Nightwind moved much swifter on the red ground than he had in the snow. From ahead came the thunder of thousands of feet and hooves. A cacophony of voices rose from thousands of throats. Randall crept quietly to the tree line to see what he had to face.

He had been worried about the huge army he heard, but once he saw what was in the clearing, he realized that kobolds were the least of his problems.

The portal stood glimmering in the clearing, perhaps four hundred feet to his left. Hundreds of kobolds were gathered in the clearing, yet they didn't seem to be entering the portal. That was the best thing Randall saw.

The worst thing he saw was the giant. Just to Randall's right the behemoth stood, gnawing on an ox. The giant must have been sixty feet tall. Its skin was light blue, its long white hair and beard were wild and matted. The creature was naked, but its long white body hair provided some coverage for its delicate bits.

"Frost giant," said Dragonwing. "It will be slow and weak from this heat, yet still too powerful for you to face. Once it crosses into the snow and cold, it will be unstoppable. We have to close the portal *now*."

Randall took a moment to look further to his right, then immediately wished he hadn't. A column of kobolds stretched as far as his eyes could see. In the distance were two more giants. If this army crossed over, the entire kingdom would surely fall.

As he retreated back into the woods, Randall noticed a flicker of movement overhead. He looked up to see something hovering beside the giant's head. It was a fluctuating flurry of purple triangles and black wedges. Randall's eyes could make no sense of it.

"A Whisperer," Dragonwing said, once the thing had moved on. "Of course, how else could kobolds and giants work together?"

"What are you talking about?" hissed Randall.

"Just go," ordered Dragonwing, "I'll explain on the way."

Randall headed back to Nightwind, and leaped into the saddle. He rode as fast as he dared through the woods.

"A Whisperer is a demon, spawned in the black void between worlds," Dragonwing began. "It poses no physical danger, but is a master of mind-magic. I have seen it once before. The demon can control the minds of lesser creatures, bending them to its will. It has other fearsome spells at its command as well. Stay away from it, if you can. Once it knows that I am here, it will be able to find us no matter how far you run. It does not see the physical world as clearly as you do, but magic appears to it as brightly as a lit candle in a dark room."

"If all goes well," said Randall, "the demon will never know we were here." He found a dense group of trees to hide Nightwind behind, and tied the horse's reins to a thick branch.

"You have a plan?" asked Dragonwing.

"A nice simple one," said Randall, "so there is less chance of anything going wrong. I'll use the alchemist's balm to disguise myself as a kobold. Then I'll head for the prism, grab it, and run through the portal. I can deactivate the prism on the other side."

"One of my wielders did something similar," said Dragonwing, "and it worked out fine."

Striding towards the tree line, Randall felt quite confident, considering his outlandish circumstances. The silver portal flickered through the trees ahead. Randall smiled; glad to be so close to his goal.

His lips froze for a moment, and then gaped open as the shock of what he was seeing set in. The portal stood tall, shining even brighter as twilight washed across the sky. On one side of it was a short pillar with a glowing prism on it. A crackling white energy beam connected prism to portal. On the other side of the portal was another short pillar with another glowing prism on it.

"Oh, no," Randall and Dragonwing said in unison.

"You said *a* prism. One." An edge of panic was creeping into Randall's voice. Two prisms meant he couldn't just grab it and head through the portal. He would have to deactivate the first one here, and then try to survive alone until Dragonwing awoke, before attempting to take the second one through.

"There can be only one," said Dragonwing. "The creation of another would have caused a great disturbance. I would have known."

"So, *what* then?" asked Randall. "Did the Whisperer get to my mind already? Is one of those prisms an illusion?"

"No. Both are really there."

"But you just said that was—"

"Impossible?" interrupted Dragonwing. "It is. This makes no sense. I...oh."

"What?"

"Nikolai! That fool!" Dragonwing was livid. "I thought I convinced him not to try."

"Who is Nikolai," Randall asked warily, "and what did he try?"

"My last wielder before you, a roving warrior from Clan Rhino. Strong and brave, to be sure, but there was one thing he just didn't understand. He wanted to break the pattern, to stop the prism from returning ever again."

"I've thought of that myself," Randall said.

"Well, don't think about it any more. Listen. Nikolai wanted to destroy the prism. I explained that it could not be broken by physical means. It was formed from powerful demonic magic. If it could have been destroyed, the elven mages would have destroyed it. Instead they did the best they could. They created me."

Randall looked up to see the first stars appear in the night sky. There were no constellations that he could recognize. In the clearing, the kobolds seemed to have settled down. Small fires were lit throughout the encampment. The smell of a thousand suppers being cooked filled the air, reminding Randall how hungry he was.

"I thought he understood," continued Dragonwing. "He said nothing more of it for those last days we were together. After the final battle, he was gravely wounded. He was going to die, and we both knew it. He approached the prism, and we said our goodbyes. That's the last thing I remember before the great sleep. He must have smashed the prism before it disappeared. I don't know how, but he broke it in two."

21

After rummaging in his pack, Randall found the small piece of bark with two words scratched on it. The first word would activate the Boom-bags that Raxus had given him. The second word was to detonate them. Randall dare not speak the words aloud, so he repeated them over and over in his mind, until he was sure he wouldn't forget.

Then he took out a small green bottle. `Feddik's Balm of Lesser Disguise', the alchemist had called it. Randall pointed to a kobold at random. It was too far away to see it very well, so he pictured in his mind one of the kobolds that he had seen much closer. "That one," he said, pulling the cork out of the small bottle. He cupped his palm and poured the balm into it. There wasn't much at all. He hoped it would be enough. He rubbed his hands together, and then rubbed the balm onto his face. The effect was immediate.

His fingers were longer, each with a sharp claw at the tip. This disguise was an illusion, so it didn't hurt like the raven transformation did. His skin was a rusty orange, covered in tiny scales. His armor was the jagged design that kobolds preferred. Too tall for a kobold, he bent his knees and hunched his back.

"Perfect," he said. "I look just like a kobold."

"But you sound like a human. Better stay silent. I'm going to be quiet as well, so the Whisperer doesn't detect my thoughts. Now go, the disguise will not last long."

Randall jogged into the clearing. Once within the light cast by the nearest campfires, he slowed to a brisk walk. The closest fire was circled by eight kobolds. They were passing a wine jug and laughing loudly. They paid Randall no heed. He passed them by, headed for a smaller fire where one old kobold sat alone.

Randall reached for a Boom-bag. The large canvas ball filled his palm. He held it to his lips. It smelled of sulphur and honey. "Nissei," he whispered.

The kobold looked up warily as Randall approached. Three small birds were cooking on a spit over the fire. The creature said something in its own language. Randall opened his mouth and pointed to it, shaking his head. He intended it to mean that he was mute, and the kobold seemed to understand.

Randall placed the Boom-bag on the ground beside the grizzled kobold. Then he held up two fingers and pointed to the roasting birds. The kobold said something angrily and shook its head. Randall shrugged, and then punched the kobold in the jaw. He wasn't worried about being seen; kobolds hit each other all the time. The lizard-man was knocked out, but Randall wrenched its neck, just to be sure.

He left the bag where it was, but took all three birds. Two went into his sack, the last he ate while he walked. He came to a small wagon laden with supplies. One whispered word later, and the wagon held an extra piece of cargo. The third Boom-bag he placed near a large group of rowdy kobolds.

That would have to be enough; he was running out of time. He spotted the nearest prism and walked towards it. It was shining too brightly to be sure, but it looked like a whole prism, not the broken half of one. Nearly a foot tall, it sat on a two-foot high ornately carved wooden pillar. A strobing white beam of energy connected it to the portal, casting eerie shadows.

It was only when he was right next to it that he realized it wasn't a prism at all. It was a glass pyramid, a cover for something smaller: one half of the Prism of Thulos.

Randall tried to remove the glass pyramid, but it was attached to the pillar somehow. He would have to smash it. He drew Dragonwing, and held the sword aloft.

"Nissera!" he shouted, hoping that he pronounced the detonation word properly. He struck the pyramid. As the glass shattered, three huge explosions rocked the night.

A shockwave sent Randall into the pillar, knocking it over. The glowing prism piece fell to the ground. Randall laid Dragonwing upon it. The illumination was immediately extinguished. The energy beam collapsed with a loud pop. Magical energy crackled like lightning along Dragonwing's blade, and then died out. The sword's silver sheen became a dull gray. It felt much heavier in Randall's hand. Now he truly was alone.

When he moved his sword, he saw nothing on the ground. The half-prism must have disappeared immediately. He patted the spot to be sure, and felt a small something sharp on his finger. It was a shard, a tiny sliver of crystal. The prism hadn't just been broken in two; it had been completely shattered. Not knowing what else to do, he placed the shard in his pouch.

He ran for the tree line. All around him, kobolds were running and screaming. Some were on fire. Bodies were scattered about.

Randall saw his hands as he ran. Not claws, hands. The disguise had worn off. He ran a little faster. With all the confusion in their camp, none of the kobolds saw him go.

22

The first hour was the worst. Running through the black forest alone. The confusion in the kobold camp wouldn't last long. Now that they knew they were not alone, that someone was actively opposing them, they would be much more vigilant. Randall expected them to charge into the forest at any time.

When he finally found Nightwind, Randall embraced the horse fiercely. He hadn't realized how much he depended on Dragonwing's companionship. The horse helped him feel slightly less alone. The horse felt smaller, and had lost its black armor. Randall's own raven armor was gone as well. He was glad for the light leather and chain armor he had gotten from Sir Darwyn. At least he wouldn't be completely defenseless.

Randall rode cautiously in the darkness, headed away from the clearing. The ground at the edge of the valley rose sharply. Soon Randall had to dismount, leading Nightwind carefully up the mountain. Trees became sparser, replaced by scrub brush and boulders.

After three hours, Randall was exhausted. He found a large rock that would hide him from the valley. Randall ate his second bird, and soon drifted into a fitful sleep.

He awoke to see the first glimmer of a scarlet sky. Wind howled ferociously across the mountainside. Curious birds flitted about in the woods below, singing their foreign songs. Randall climbed the rock he had hidden behind. There he sat, eating the last of the birds he had taken last night.

He had an unobstructed view of the clearing. The kobolds seemed much more organized than they had before. They stood in orderly lines on either side of the clearing, leaving a wide path to the portal. On the other side of that path was a giant, the one who had swatted Randall out of the air when he first arrived. Before, the giant would have had to slouch a bit to get through the portal. When Randall deactivated the prism shard, the portal must have shrunk to half its size. The giant obviously didn't want to squeeze through it now that it was only twenty-five feet high. The behemoth lashed out, knocking down the nearest kobolds with its flailing.

Randall smiled a hollow smile. This was his last chance, and he was powerless. Once the giant got through, the kingdom was lost. This was it. Everything that he had gone through was for nothing.

Under the weight of his despair, he felt a lightness. Was he accepting his loss? No, he actually felt lighter. The weight on his back had lessened. Dawn spread her crimson fingers to the horizon, and Randall felt inexplicably happy.

"Well, you're not dead," said Dragonwing. "That's something."

"Sword! You're back!" said Randall, voice cracking. He drew blade from scabbard. The dull gray steel had returned to its former silver sheen. Randall wiped a tear from his eye. "I thought I was finally rid of you!"

"I missed you too," said Dragonwing. "How are we doing?"

"We're out of time. That giant is going through any minute."

In the clearing, the giant ceased its tantrum. A purple something flickered in front of its head. The Whisperer was trying to control the beast. In a few moments the giant would go through whether it wanted to or not.

"I know I said I wouldn't do it again," said Randall, "but there is only one thing left to do. We have to transform into a raven again. We swoop down there, grab the pillar, and fly through the portal."

"I'm too weak!" protested Dragonwing. "I just woke up, I don't have enough power."

"There is no choice," said Randall. "We do this now, or we die trying."

23

Raven swooped down from the mountainside, and glided over the trees. The red sky had been replaced by angry violet storm clouds. Thunder echoed across the heavens. Licks of lightning lashed above the great bird as it glided down into the valley.

The knight inside left the flying to Raven, but had two clear orders. First: grab the glowing thing. Second: fly through the silver hole. Easy.

The rain hit like a wall of water. Raven struggled with suddenly wet feathers, dipping for a moment into the canopy. As Raven flew into the clearing, the giant fell to all fours and began to crawl. Raven was flying low, just out of reach of the kobold's spears. Flapping. Flapping. Almost there.

The giant's head and shoulders were through the portal. There was no way that Raven could fit through. Talons extended, it grabbed the log with the glowing glass on top.

"Up, up!" shouted the knight inside.

Raven grabbed the pillar and rose, narrowly avoiding the giant's back. The white beam that connected shard to portal seemed to pull at Raven's talons, slowing his escape.

"Fly for the mountain ahead," cried the knight inside.

Raven flew with a great effort, tugging the beam behind him. Up ahead, an indigo flicker exploded into a purple and black morass of shapes. The Whisperer had found him at last.

Ethereal black snakes streamed from the Whisperer to embrace Raven. The spells were powerful; Raven never had a chance to escape.

Randall felt the feathers falter. Suddenly the raven consciousness was gone, and he had to pilot his strange body alone. He set sights upon the mountain ahead, and flapped with all his might. The pillar seemed to drag at his talons, but still he flew. The Whisperer disappeared from behind and coalesced in his path once again. Randall climbed high to avoid it.

The demon called the very lightning from the sky into itself, and spewed out a multitude of vile bolts. A few of the black streaks hit the raven, and that was it. Dragonwing was senseless, and the feathers began to retreat into Randall's pores.

In a flurry of feathers and curses, Randall streaked into the side of the mountain. Giant bird transformed into horse and man, and both hit the rocks at high velocity. They slid down the rocks until they landed on an eight-foot wide platform. The stones they knocked loose continued on their way, causing a great avalanche in the valley below.

Randall drew Dragonwing. Something was wrong; the sword was flickering from gray to silver. Twenty feet further along the platform lay the pillar and the glowing shard, its glass cover shattered on the cliff. Randall staggered forward.

Between him and the shard, a cluster of purple triangles and black wedges appeared. The Whisperer erupted in a cascade of light, casting a powerful spell. Randall jabbed ahead with his sword, and Dragonwing's magic dissolved the Whisperer. It was too late. The spell had already taken hold.

Randall began to weep. There was no hope. Something important had been lost, but he had no idea what it was. He was so confused. He couldn't even remember why he was here.

"Da da dur," stammered Dragonwing. "Shard. Touch it."

Randall glanced down at the clearing. The giant's buttocks and legs were protruding from the portal. As confused as he was, he remembered a few things. If he closed the portal, he would be stuck here forever. He could save the kingdom, but he could never return. Was his life more important than a million innocents? It was not. There was never really any choice.

The Raven Knight laid his blade across the sliver of prism. The last bit of Dragonwing's magic was used up to extinguish the shard. As the portal closed, the giant was cut in half.

*

The Whisperer's spell cut deep. Randall forgot about his quest, he forgot about Dragonwing, he forgot everything. He was just a man on a mountain. After a while, he grabbed his horse's reins and began to walk. He took the narrow alpine path, around the mountain to the other side. Once the terrain was safe, he mounted the horse. The young man rode through the valley and past the mountains beyond. He rode and rode.

After a time, he found a grove where game was plentiful and the soil was pure. This was as good a place to settle as any. He had no recollection of what he had lost. No recollection of what he had done.

After a week of work, a shelter took shape. The man made spears to hunt with. The man plowed earth to sow his seeds. The man made a life for himself. He had only one decoration: a dull old sword with a winged hand-guard and a bone hilt. The lonely man hung his decoration over his doorway and left it there. The decoration became brittle, and covered over with rust.

The man lived a life of peace in his lonely corner of the red mountains. Ignorance truly was bliss.

EPILOGUE

Days became weeks. Weeks became months. The months rolled on. Life wasn't easy, and a hard life makes a hard man. Innocence and humor, those last vestiges of youth, were long gone. The man's heart had grown cold, but still he clung to life.

He had been trailing the boar for three days. It was a big one, with tusks the size of his forearm. The beast's path seemed chaotic at first, but the man had discerned a pattern. Near the creek where the boar liked to drink was a gnarled tree. The man crouched on a low branch, spear poised, waiting for the boar to pass underneath.

The proud beast grew thirsty, and came to drink. The man flowed from the tree like liquid death. His first strike was true, but the beast was too strong to fall right away. The boar flailed right and left, coughing out blood from its collapsed lung. One of its tusks tore the man's arm from wrist to elbow. The man used his good arm to drive the spear deeper, pinning the boar to the ground. After a few more spasms, the beast died.

Blood gushed from the maimed arm, staining the ground below. The man knew that if he kept bleeding like this, he would soon be dead. His very life was spilling into the dirt and mud.

His head was filled with a thickness that made it hard to think. The same thing happened whenever he tried to think of his life before. He knew that he had lived another life. He knew that he had lost something important. Whenever he tried too hard to remember, the pressure in his brain became too much, and he had to back off. This was like that, but he did know one thing: it was time to drink from that small bottle that he had been carrying all this time.

He uncorked the bottle, and drank half of the sweet liquid. He managed to re-cork the bottle before the weakness from all the lost blood overtook him. He collapsed in a heap.

*

Opening his eyes, he saw a black bird streak across the morning sky. Why did that seem familiar? Did he dream he was a raven, flying free in the blue sky?

He shook the nonsense from his head and stood. The air smelled of blood and death. His weakness and the stench forced him back to his knees. He retched onto the dirt; expelling things he didn't remember eating. The vomit splashed back onto his arms, and he noticed the wounded one. No longer ruined and bleeding, the cut in his arm had closed over, and was now covered with an ugly scar.

The thickness in his head ebbed for a moment, and he remembered a little old fellow giving him the bottle. It was some kind of healing potion. He almost recalled more, but then the thickness returned.

No time for nonsense, the man got to work. He gathered vines and branches, and built a crude sled to drag the great boar back home. All his tools for cleaning and gutting a carcass were back at the shelter, and he had to get the boar there before it began to rot.

The beast was heavy, and the trek was hard. It would be worth all the trouble. The boar pelt would be useful in the coming winter, and the meat would last a good long time.

Once he reached the grove, and saw his humble shelter in the distance, the man smiled. It wasn't much, but it was home. The suns were low in the sky. As they fell, the red sun lit some leaves with an orange glow. The yellow sun made other leaves look like they were forged from gold. The man's twin shadows stretched far ahead. The pre-twilight was always a magic time, and it only lasted for a brief moment. One of the suns caught something at the shelter, reflecting a flash of light back at the man.

He let go of the sled and readied his spear. Something was wrong. It was his home, and he knew how to sneak up on it better than anyone. He crept behind tall grasses until he was right beside his hovel of mud and wood. Peering through the grass, expecting an intruder, he sighed with relief when he saw what it was.

Above his doorway, the shining something reflected the dying light one last time. The man stood, unafraid. The thickness in his head began to fade.

The thing hanging above the doorway had become something of a talisman, a good-luck charm of sorts. Every time he walked through the doorway, he reached up to touch it. Even when he didn't know what it was, he knew he loved it. At first, the steel part was dull gray, and the bone part was bright white. Over time, the bone had become dull and desiccated. The steel had quickly become webbed over with rust, and lately had dissolved into an orange and brown ghost of its former shape. Now it was whole once again.

Memories came back in a flood, threatening to knock him to his knees. Newfound strength kept him on his feet.

Randall walked to the crude hut and tore the sword from the twigs that held it in place.

The Raven Knight held Dragonwing aloft, silver blade silhouetted against the gloaming sky.

END